Finding H.F.

Finding H.F.

Julia Watts

alyson books
los angeles | new york

MANUFACTURED IN THE UNITED STATES OF AMERICA.

THIS TRADE PAPERBACK ORIGINAL IS PUBLISHED BY
ALYSON PUBLICATIONS,
P.O. BOX 4371, LOS ANGELES, CA 90078-4371.
DISTRIBUTION IN THE UNITED KINGDOM BY
TURNAROUND PUBLISHER SERVICES LTD.,
UNIT 3, OLYMPIA TRADING ESTATE, COBURG ROAD, WOOD GREEN,
LONDON N22 6TZ ENGLAND.

FIRST EDITION: OCTOBER 2001

01 02 03 04 05 a 10 9 8 7 6 5 4 3 2 1

ISBN 1-55583-622-4

LIBRARY OF CONGRESS CATALOGING-IN-PUBLICATION DATA
WATTS, JULIA, 1969—
FINDING H.F. / BY JULIA WATTS.—1ST ED.
ISBN 1-55583-622-4
1. LESBIAN TEENAGERS—FICTION. 2. SOUTHERN STATES—FICTION.
I. TITLE: FINDING H.F. II. TITLE.
PS3573.A868 F56 2001
813'.54—DC21   2001031596

CREDITS
COVER DESIGN BY MATT SAMS.
COVER PHOTOGRAPHY BY PHOTODISC INC.

"God gave Noah the rainbow sign, don't you see?"

—traditional hymn

Part One:

The Flood

ONE

When somebody asks what my initials stand for, I always say the same thing: "You promise not to laugh if I tell you?" Whoever it is always promises, and then when I tell them, they bust out laughing anyway.

I used to get mad when kids laughed at my name—I even got into fights about it on the playground in grade school—but now I don't blame people for laughing. My name *is* funny. It fits me about as well as the blue coat Memaw bought me when I was in third grade. When I tried it on, she looked at how the sleeves hung down long and loose like the arms on an orangutan and said, "You'll grow into it." And four years later I did.

I guess Memaw hopes I'll grow into my name the same way I grew into that blue coat, but I'll tell you right now, it ain't gonna happen. I know what Memaw was thinking when she named me—here comes the name, promise not to laugh—Heavenly Faith. (And don't think I didn't hear you laughing just now.) She was thinking, *If I give my grandbaby a name that puts her close to the Lord, she won't make the same mistakes her momma did. She'll put her faith in heaven and not let the sins of this earth drag her down.*

Well, let's just say the name didn't take.

It's not like I'm a bad girl exactly, but I'm sure not the girl Memaw was picturing when she came up with that crazy name. And I'm not the girl she thought I would grow up to be when she was filling my head with every Bible story and hymn that ever was. She dragged me to Sunday school, vacation Bible school, and services at the Morgan Freewill Baptist Tabernacle until I got so big that she couldn't drag me anymore.

Of course, when I was little I didn't hate all that church stuff. Some of the Bible stories were fun in a blood-and-guts kinda way, and I used to love the picture in the Sunday school room of all the animals lined up to get on Noah's Ark. And the cookies and Kool-Aid at Bible school always tasted good.

But the thing is, I never believed those Bible stories were real any more than I believed *The Poky Little Puppy* was real when Memaw read it to me. I didn't believe in those Bible things any more than I believed in talking dogs that ate strawberry shortcake. That's what makes my name so funny. Heavenly Faith, my foot! If I can't see it, hear it, smell it, touch it, or taste it, I don't believe in it.

That's why I make everybody call me H.F. Well, everybody but Memaw. I let her call me Faith, without the "Heavenly" part, because I feel sorry for her. She didn't get the granddaughter she asked for, so I let her use part of the name she gave me as a consolation prize...like on game shows when you don't win the big money so they give you a case of Rice-A-Roni to make you feel better.

Don't get me wrong. I know Memaw loves me. I know it because I see it and hear it everyday—the way she mends my ratty blue jeans instead of making me wear dresses, the way she lets me eat macaroni and cheese straight out of the pan. Even how she rubs the top of my head and says, "I swear, I don't know what I'm gonna do with you" is full of love. But I know I'm not the model granddaughter she asked for. She says she's glad of one thing, though: At least I'm not boy-crazy.

If Memaw knew the truth—that I'm girl-crazy instead—I don't know what she'd do. Pray and cry and try to get me "cured," I reckon. One thing's for sure: She'd never understand it, and neither would most people in Morgan, Kentucky, which ain't exactly San Francisco, if you know what I mean. So to keep from making trouble for me and other people, I keep my mouth shut and try to feel good that at least I won't break Memaw's heart by getting pregnant before I finish high school, which is what my momma did.

The fact that my mother got pregnant when she was 15 years old is one of the few things I know about her, and of course, the only reason I know that much is because it's why I'm here.

Here's what I do know about her: Her name is Sondra Louise Simms, and she was the youngest—by 16 years—of three children. Uncle Bobby, who eats supper with Memaw and me every week or so, told me he barely knew his little sister.

"She wasn't nothin' but a baby the whole time I was livin' at home," he told me one night as he sat at the kitchen table drinking his third cup of coffee. "And then I went off and joined the Army. By the time I got back home, I didn't hardly recognize her."

I'd love to ask Mom's other brother, Gary, about her. But he lives up in Ohio, so we don't get a chance to talk much.

Most of the pictures Memaw has are from when Momma was little. She was a pretty, dark-eyed baby who looks real serious in all the pictures—not all gummy, drooly smiles like a lot of babies. If the photographer was making silly faces at her or telling her to watch the funny puppet, she wasn't having any of it. In every picture she looks as serious as a little funeral director.

There's just one picture of Momma from when she was older. Memaw says Momma was 15 when Uncle Bobby snapped that picture, so I don't know if I was already growing inside her. If she was pregnant, she wasn't too far gone, because her belly don't bulge at all under her tight jeans. She's standing in front of Memaw's little white frame house, wearing a black Van Halen T-shirt and holding a cigarette. Her hair is thick and dark and wavy, not like mine, which is stick-straight and dishwater blond.

I always try to see some resemblance between her and me, but I can't. Whoever my daddy was, he must have been a plain-looking, blue-eyed skinny boy, since that's what I look like, right down to the "boy" part.

In the picture, though, my mother doesn't look like a boy at all. She has curves everywhere she's supposed to have them and these long, fringy eyelashes. She looks pretty but mad, like the last thing she wants to be doing is having her picture took, and the last place she wants to be is hanging around this old house in Morgan, with all of Memaw's concrete frogs and geese in the tiny front yard.

And I guess this was the last place she wanted to be. Momma left Memaw and me when she was 16, the same age I am now.

Every time I ask Memaw about the day Momma left, she says the same thing: "That day like to killed me."

When my mother told Memaw she was pregnant, Memaw planned everything out so she could stay in school. I wasn't due until July, so she could have me during summer vacation and then be back at school to start her sophomore year. Momma lived up to part of the bargain: She finished her freshman year and had me in the summer. She even went back to start her sophomore year. But the day after my mother's 16th birthday, Memaw knocked on her bedroom door and found her and all of her belongings gone—everything but the little white Bible Memaw gave her for her 12th birthday. All of Memaw's plans were shot to hell in that instant, and I was still snoozing away in my crib.

Memaw could've called the police, but she didn't. She says she figured Momma would show in a few days, out of money and ready for a hot meal. When she didn't, Memaw asked Uncle Bobby to call a guy he knew from the Army, a private investigator up in Richmond. He tracked Momma down to a town in South Carolina once, but she disappeared before he could talk to her.

Memaw's money started disappearing too, into the pockets of the private investigator, and pretty soon she had to choose between paying out money on the chance she would find my mother or paying to feed and clothe me. "So," Memaw always says, "I chose you. But I never stopped praying for your mother."

I only know this much because I kept driving Memaw crazy with questions until she had to answer them. Maybe I ought to be a private investigator myself.

Most of the time, though, we don't talk about Momma, because, like Memaw says, there's no point in talking about her. She hasn't showed up in 16 years, which means she's not that interested in us, right?

But I'm a curious person. I can't help thinking about her, and sometimes I wonder if she's even a tiny bit curious about me. I've made Memaw promise that if she ever hears anything from her—a letter, postcard, anything—she has to show it to me. But there's been nothing.

It's not like I spend all my time pining for my mother. Most days I don't even think about her. Or I just think about her once or twice. I do have a life.

Unlike Momma, I fully intend to graduate from high school. I'm finishing up my sophomore year at Morgan High, and except for math, I like the book-learning part of school just fine. It's the people I can't stand—not all the people, but the cheer-leaders and jocks and the people who walk around and every step they take says, *My daddy has money, and you don't even know who your daddy is.*

But it's not the money thing or even the illegitimate thing that makes me such an outcast—it's that the cheerleaders and jocks and popular kids know I'm different. Different on the inside. Like lions on nature shows that sniff out which gazelle is ripest for the picking, those people can sniff out difference—and it's a smell they hate.

I guess I'm lucky, though, because I'm not the only one in school who's different. I don't have to be a lonely gazelle limping along while the lions stalk me. I've got Bo for a friend, and bless his heart, he's got it a lot rougher than I do. The sissy boys always have it harder than the tomboys. If you're a boyish girl, other girls just snub you, but if you're a girlish boy, other boys beat the living hell out of you. Believe me, I've picked Bo up off the pavement more times than I can count.

Sometimes a nice teacher comes along and stops the fight—not that you could really call it a fight, because it's always four or more guys against Bo. But most teachers pretend not to notice, because they're just older versions of the boys who are kicking the crap out of the "faggot." They also smell that Bo's different, and they think he deserves a good butt whipping because of it.

But I gotta hand it to Bo. He gets his licks in—not with his fists but with his brains. Like the hot pepper incident, for example.

Bo's daddy is one of those macho men who likes to prove how tough he is by eating peppers so hot they make blisters on your gums. Back in the fall, after the football boys had beat him up pretty bad, Bo snuck into his daddy's hot pepper supply and stole a few of the ones his daddy grows special—some Mexican kind that's supposed to be the hottest pepper on earth.

Me and Bo put the peppers in a blender and chopped them up till they turned into this scary-looking nuclear-green juice. Bo sneaked into the football locker room one Friday afternoon before a game and dabbed a little bit of the pepper juice onto every jock strap he could find.

Since Bo is in the marching band, he got to see it all. That night, the Morgan High School Rebels came running out on the field for the big game against the Taylorsville Blue Devils, only to fall to the ground, screaming and digging at their crotches like crazed animals. The game was canceled, and the team ran over each other and mowed down a few cheerleaders in their rush to get to the showers.

I was scared to death that somebody would figure out Bo did it and kill him, but he said I was giving the jocks too much credit. I remember him grinning extra wide, even though his lip was still split from his last beating. "I reckon I showed them sumbitches that there's some things worse than a busted lip," he laughed. "Even if they did find out and kill me, it just might be worth it."

Right now I'm sitting in the institutional-green hall here at dear old Morgan High, waiting for Bo to get out of band practice. Me and Bo spend most afternoons together, doing a whole lot of nothing.

Bo's got a car—or what passes for one—a beat-up old brown Ford Escort he bought with money he saved from playing music in different churches. So most afternoons we just ride around. Sometimes we stop at the Dixie Diner for a chili dog or the G&J Drive-In for a root beer, but mostly we just drive the back roads and talk, staying out as long as we can without getting in trouble for being late for supper.

For Bo, the trouble he'd get in would be deep. Like I said, Bo's dad is a tough guy, and I'm sure he wasn't thinking he had a sissy on his hands when he named his firstborn son Pierre Beauregard, after his favorite Confederate general. Bo's younger brother, Nathan, is just like Bo's daddy. He's just in the eighth grade, but he already wears a "Confederate States of America" belt buckle. Bo says he wonders if the hospital made a mistake when he was born and gave him to the wrong family.

The band room door swings open, and all the little band nerds come trooping out, Bo along with them. His blond hair is carefully arranged in short, neat waves around his heart-shaped, acne-free face. In a testosterone-soaked town like Morgan, Bo is almost too pretty for his own good. When he spots me, he gives me a little wave with his flute case. He's the only boy flute player in the band, and I wouldn't be surprised if he was the only boy flute player in all of Kentucky.

Bo is wearing this shiny green vest over a collarless shirt, looking all snazzy. He buys all his clothes from catalogs with the money he gets from his church gigs. He says he wouldn't go to a dog's funeral wearing the clothes you can buy in Morgan.

"Hey, sugar!" He waves his little flute case at me. "You ready to go ridin' around?"

"Sure." I reach down and pick up my schoolbag off the floor, but when I stand up and see the person in front of me, I freeze like a possum in headlights.

Wendy Cook is the most beautiful girl I've seen in my life, and that includes TV and movie actresses. She has long, curly, red hair that stands out from her pretty face like a burning bush. She's always wearing these long, flowered dresses with boots or clogs, and she's always carrying a book with her—not a schoolbook, but a book she's reading for fun.

Wendy and her parents moved here last year when her dad got a job teaching at Randall College, Morgan's only institution of higher learning, which is run by people who are about as Jesus-crazy as Memaw is. The Cooks lived in Pennsylvania before, and I don't think Wendy's very happy in Morgan. How could she be? One of the biggest strikes a person can have against somebody in this town is them not being from around here.

It's totally ridiculous for me to have a crush on Wendy. Like that poem we read in English the other day said, "Let me count the ways." It's totally ridiculous because (1) she's a girl and so am I; (2) her dad's a college professor, and I'm going to be the only member of my family who even graduated from high school; (3) she's been to New York City and overseas, and I've never been farther away from home than Lexington, (4) she...

"Me and H.F. was about to go ridin' around," Bo is saying to Wendy, who I've been staring at like a crazy person for I don't know how long. "Wanna come with us?"

I can't believe he's doing this. If I so much as lay eyes on the girl, my tongue turns to rubber in my mouth. How does he expect me to talk to her?

"A tempting offer, but I've got to head over to Randall for my piano lesson."

I'm relieved and disappointed at the same time.

"Well, you have fun tinkling them ivories, sugar," Bo says.

Wendy crinkles up her freckled nose. "I'll try. Well...see you, Bo...H.F."

"See ya," Bo says. I manage to say "See ya" too, but not until Wendy is already out the door.

Two

"You sure got it bad for Pippi Longstocking," Bo says as we're pulling out of the parking lot of the G&J Drive-In.

"She does *not* look like Pippi Longstocking." I'm trying to sound annoyed, but I'm laughing.

"Who're you tryin' to kid? All them freckles and that red hair? Put her in pigtails and stick her finger in a light socket, and she'd be Pippi Longstocking."

"It's bad enough I've got a useless crush on this girl," I say. "Now you've gotta make fun of me for it."

"I'm not making fun of you...I'm making fun of her." I watch him spot a sign marked DEER CREEK ROAD. "Hey, let's see where this road goes," he says, making a sudden turn.

"I bet it goes past trailers and churches and cow fields like every other dang road in this county. I'd be real surprised if we landed in front of the Taj Mahal." I look out the window as we pass a trailer with children in their underwear playing in the front yard. "Anyway, why are you making fun of Wendy? I thought you liked her fine."

"Shoot, H.F., I don't have nothin' against her. It's just like you said: It's a useless crush. And if it's useless, I don't feel like I ought to be encouragin' it."

"You're probably right." We pass a little concrete-block church with a sign that says, THE CHURCH OF THE LIVING GOD IN JESUS' HOLY NAME, THE ONE TRUE WAY WITHOUT ARGUMENT. I crack up.

"What's so funny?"

"Did you see the name of that church?"

"Yeah, so?"

"I just think it's funny...all the people in them little churches start arguing about scripture and get all pissed off at each other. Then some people split off and start a new church and give it a name a mile long so everybody will know they're not them blasphemers at the old church. You know, like they call it 'The One True Church of Jesus Christ, Not to Be Confused With That Other Church of Jesus Christ, Because All the People Who Go There Are Gonna Burn in Hell.'"

Bo laughs. "You're awful, H.F. You're the one who's gonna burn in hell."

"If you're gonna start preachin' hellfire and brimstone, you might as well drive me home. Memaw's the one that's stuck with the job of savin' my soul. And besides, if what them church people say is right, you'll be right next to me in hell, shovelin' coal and complainin' about how the heat makes your clothes wrinkle." I look out the window, and a cow standing by an electric fence peers up at me with sad brown eyes. "Hmm. You know, I was just thinkin', when I get a useless crush on some girl like Wendy, the only thing I do is talk to you about it. I'd be too scared to act on the kinda crushes I get. But you never even talk about yours."

Bo and me have been best friends since we were eight years old, and in all that time, he's never told me about a single person he has a crush on. As early as second grade, I was getting all goo-goo-eyed over the pretty student teachers that got sent over from Randall College to practice their skills on a room full of rowdy kids. I'd spend hours talking to Bo about Miss Tammy, the student teacher, making up crazy, romantic stories about what her life outside school must be like. Bo's been listening to my overactive fantasy life for eight years now, but he's never given me so much as a glimpse into his own.

13

Come to think of it, Bo has never come right out and told me he likes boys. He'll say things like, "bein' the way I am" or "not bein' a real masculine type of person," but he's never plainly said he likes boys in general, let alone one boy in particular. Instead he rattles on about stuff like how much he just loves that new Celine Dion song. I don't know who he thinks he's kidding. If you're a boy who lives in a place like Morgan, and you just can't stop talking about how *fabulous* that new Celine Dion single is, guess what, buddy: You've done come out of the closet.

"Well, I guess if there was anybody around here that was worth havin' a crush on, I'd talk about it," Bo says. Honestly, I don't see why he has to be so mysterious all the time.

"Well, when you get that music scholarship to the University of Kentucky, I bet there'll be somebody up there worth fallin' for."

"*If* I get a music scholarship to UK." Bo's little hands grip the steering wheel tighter. "There's lots of competition for them scholarships...people from all over the state who've had lots better music teachers than some sissy little piece of white trash from Morgan County."

"Hey, now. Don't beat yourself up. That's the football team's job."

Bo grins for a second, but then his face gets all serious again. "Well, even if I do get a scholarship, it still might not be enough money. Daddy wouldn't pay a plugged nickel for me to go to UK, unless I was goin' there to play on the basketball team. And if I even mention the word 'college,' he starts saying, 'You think you're better'n me?' "

"I guess 'yes' would be the wrong answer."

"Wrong enough to get me an ass whippin', and, like you said, that's the football team's job."

Bo may have a momma and a daddy, but his day-to-day life

is a lot worse than mine. His momma works overtime at the bandage factory over in Taylorsville, and his daddy was a logger until he hurt his back. Now he's a drinker and a yeller and sometimes a hitter. Bo tries to stay out of his way.

I know Memaw doesn't understand a whole lot about me, but she don't yell much, and she's never hit me. Even if she found out I like girls, I don't believe she'd beat me.

Deer Creek Road comes to a dead end. The pavement just stops, and there's a cleared-out space to turn your car around. A lot of roads around here turn from pavement to gravel to dirt, but not many roads just stop. Bo pulls into the turn-around spot. "So what do you wanna do now?"

I look outside. Just in front of us is a stretch of woods. The sun is shining in yellow beams through the light green leaves of the trees. I remember hearing somebody say that's what the light shining through stained glass windows in a church is supposed to look like. "You wanna walk around a little while?"

"You don't reckon it'll be muddy, do you?"

I look at Bo's perfectly arranged little waves of blond hair. I swear, it's like his number one concern in life is being well groomed. The boy irons his jeans, for crying out loud. "What's the matter, Beauregard? Afraid of messin' up your snazzy new shoes?"

"Excuse me, sugar, but some people take pride in their personal appearance." He looks down at my clothes and curls up his lip. "Yep...and some people throw on any ol' thing that'll cover their private parts."

Bo's right about the way I look. When it comes to clothes, I couldn't be less like a teenage girl. Most mornings I get dressed before I even turn on the light in my room. I shuck off my pajamas, grab some socks and underwear out of the top drawer, a T-shirt out of the middle drawer, and a pair of jeans from the bottom. Some water on my face, a quick brush over my hair and teeth, and I'm ready to go. Sometimes I've been in school a couple of hours before I look down and notice what I've got on.

There's a path through the trees. In the mud, which has dried enough not to hurt Bo's beloved footwear too much, there are tracks from some man's huge clodhoppers and dainty hoof-prints left by a deer. I head down the trail.

"Where do you think you're goin'?"

"I thought we'd follow this trail a ways."

"God, I hate it when you decide you're Daniel Boone." Bo steps cautiously over a tree root.

"That's *Danielle* Boone to you," I say.

Bo rolls his eyes, but he still follows me. For some reason he always does.

The sunlight pours down through the trees, warm and bright like melted butter. "You know, this place is probably eat up with snakes," Bo says.

"April's early for snakes."

"Yeah, well, with my luck, I'll probably run into a snake that's an early riser."

"Hush a minute. I hear somethin'."

"Omigod, what?" Bo whips his head around.

I close my eyes and hear a soft whooshing. "Water. Over the hill, I think. Come on...let's go see."

Bo sighs as we climb the hill. "Lord, you're worse than my daddy. You know, he tried to take me deer huntin' one time. He made me put on this ugly old camouflage jumpsuit and took me out to the woods. Then he handed me this bottle of nasty-smellin' stuff to smear all over me. I said, 'What's this?' And he said, 'It attracts the deers...it smells like deer piss.' I was like, 'Excuse me? I don't think so! I wouldn't wanna smell like deer piss even if I *was* a deer.' I don't think other deers would find that smell so attractive, do you? Oh...my...God."

He says it at the same time I do. We've hit the top of the hill, and what we see below us makes our jaws drop. It's a creek, all right—Deer Creek would be my guess—but at the near end of the creek is what must be a ten-foot waterfall sending a perfect white spray onto the rocks below. It's so beautiful, it makes my stomach flip-flop.

I run to the creek, shuck off my sneakers and socks, roll up my jeans, and step into the cool, clear water. It's a warm day for April—warm enough for the sunshine to have knocked the chill off the water. I love the gentle rush of the creek over my feet and ankles, the feel of the mud squishing between my toes.

Bo inspects a big rock, dusts it off, and sits down on it. He laughs at me. "You look about six years old in there."

I splash some water toward him, and he ducks, laughing. "I feel about six years old. Except I feel even better than when I was six. You know what I think, Bo? I think us findin' this place is a sign."

"Oh, you and your signs," he says. "Ain't nobody believes in signs except old grannies and the girls who get raised by 'em."

It's true that Memaw taught me to believe in signs—in little things that happen because something big is about to happen. The best example of Memaw following a sign is from when she was a young girl, just after she married my papaw. Papaw was off fighting in the war, and Memaw was staying with her mother and daddy, helping to take care of the housework and her younger brothers and sisters.

One evening Memaw was taking the wash off the line when she heard the rooster crowing from the henhouse. "Now, every-body knows," Memaw always says, "that when a rooster crows of an evenin', it means somebody's fixin' to die."

Memaw dropped her washing on the ground, ran to the hen-house, grabbed the old rooster, and wrung its neck. The next morning she got a telegram saying her husband had been injured in combat and would be coming home after they let him out of the hospital. Later, when Papaw came home, him and Memaw figured out the time when he had been shot: right when that rooster crowed.

Now, I know I already told you I don't believe any of that loaves-and-fishes and water-to-wine stuff, but I do believe this. Papaw had to get his foot amputated because of getting shot, but because Memaw killed that rooster when it crowed, he lived to come home and see his three children grow up to be teenagers before he died. Bo can call me superstitious all he wants, but that's what I believe: Sometimes nature puts a sign in front of you, and when it does, you'd better do what it tells you.

"Findin' this place *is* a sign...a good sign," I say, running my toes over the smooth creek pebbles. "Think about it. Ever since you turned 16, we've been ridin' around every day after school, drivin' and drivin' but goin' nowhere. Bo, today we finally went someplace. After months of drivin' we finally found a destination, don't you see?"

"Well, I like this place too, and I'm glad we found it. But it ain't a sign, because except for the ones on the road that say STOP and NO RIGHT TURN and EAT AT JOE'S, there ain't no such thing as signs."

"Well, you can say it ain't a sign all you want, but I know it is, and I know what it's a sign of. Bo, our lives are finally goin' someplace. And just look around you at the water and the trees and the sky...it's gonna be someplace beautiful."

Bo smiles. I can tell he's trying not to roll his eyes at me. "Well, I sure hope you're right, H.F."

I can feel the sun pouring down on me, the water lapping at my ankles, and the earth under my feet, and I know I'm right. "Of course I'm right, Bo. You know what I'm gonna do?"

"I'm scared to ask."

"I'm gonna start talkin' to Wendy Cook."

"Now, H.F., you've gotta be careful. Bein' the way you are…"

"I'll be careful. I'm not gonna tell her how I feel or nothin'…but I figure maybe I can be her friend, and that's better than nothin', right?"

"Yeah." Bo grins. "Of course, you're gonna have to learn how to make words come out of your mouth when you see her. As far as I can tell, seein' Wendy Cook is the only thing on God's green earth guaranteed to shut you up."

"Well, that's all gonna change today. Today I'm gonna take my shyness and wash it away under that waterfall."

I start running through the creek toward the waterfall, with Bo running alongside me on land, hollering, "H.F., you can't stand under that waterfall! You'll get pneumonia! And you can't go home to your memaw with your clothes all wet."

He's right about the clothes. I climb onto the bank and strip off my jeans and T-shirt, then step back in the water, wearing nothing but the white cotton "granny panties" Memaw buys for me and the bra I'm almost too flat-chested to need.

"You put your clothes back on!" Bo yelps. "What would somebody say if they walked up and saw me here with you in just your drawers?"

I strike a bathing-beauty pose and grin at Bo. "They'd say, 'I didn't know you had it in you, stud!'"

Bo's face turns the color of the pickled beets Memaw is always trying to make me eat. I run into the waterfall. The rush of cold water makes me gasp, but when I take in my next gulp of misty air, I feel awake and alive. I close my eyes and stretch up my arms, letting the cold water beat down on me, washing all my fears downstream.

But I can't stay under the water for long. My teeth chatter as I wrestle with my jeans, trying to pull them up over my wet skin, which is not cooperating.

"Lord a-mighty, H.F., your lips have turned blue." Bo takes off his vest and hands it to me. "I told you you'd catch pneumonia."

I slip on Bo's vest and hug it to my chest. "I d-don't have pneu-m-monia. The walk back to the c-car will warm me up just f-fine." My teeth are chattering so bad it's hard to talk. I realize now that I should've stripped off my bra and panties too, before I got under the waterfall, even though me being buck naked would've embarrassed the living daylights out of Bo. But at least that way my underwear would've been warm and dry instead of clammy and sticking to the parts of my body that hate being cold the most.

Freezing as I am, though, I still feel good. There's something to be said for not hanging back, for jumping right in and doing what you feel like doing. Bo may think I'm crazy, but if I had it to do again, I'd still go stand under that waterfall. But this time, I'd do it naked.

THREE

I hate milk, but Memaw makes me drink it. I've just sat down at the dinette in the kitchen, after sneaking into my room to change my underwear, and there's this huge tumbler of milk at my place. "Lord, Memaw, how much does this glass hold? A half gallon?"

Memaw is fixing my plate at the stove. Like always, her steel-gray hair is pulled back in a bun, and she has on one of the plain zipper-front dresses she runs up for herself on her Singer sewing machine. "Them glasses was on sale over at the Dollar General Store. I like big glasses."

"It seems to me you might as well just put a jug of milk on the table and stick a straw in it."

Memaw shakes her head good-naturedly as she sets down my plate. "You're a sight," she says. On my plate is one of her usual suppers: pinto beans, fried potatoes, and cabbage. The corn bread is already on the table.

After Memaw fixes her own plate, she settles down across from me. Her big glass is filled with the iced tea she makes, which is so thick and sweet, it's like drinking maple syrup.

Memaw definitely has a sweet tooth. She always has to have something sugary before she goes to bed. Usually it's a dish of ice cream, but sometimes if there's leftover biscuits, she'll take one and split it and squirt Hershey's syrup all over it. Memaw isn't fat exactly, but she's well padded, like an overstuffed arm-chair. When I was little, I used to listen to more Bible stories than I really wanted to hear because I didn't want to leave Memaw's comfy lap.

"So how's your little boyfriend?" Memaw always calls Bo my boyfriend because she knows it drives me pure and tee crazy.

"He's not my boyfriend," I say around a mouthful of cabbage.

"Well, he's a boy and he's your friend, ain't he? Even if he does got ruffles on his drawers." She takes a swig of tea before she says, "And don't talk with food in your mouth."

I think about telling Memaw about the waterfall Bo and me found but decide to keep it a secret.

"You got lessons tonight?" She always calls homework "lessons," just like she calls lunch "dinner."

"Not too many. About an hour's worth."

"You wanna help me blow some eggs after you wash the dishes?"

"Sure, why not?"

Yeah, I know I've got to explain about the "blowing eggs" thing. It almost sounds like something dirty instead of something you'd sit around doing with your memaw.

You see, Memaw's always doing these crafty things; I call them her infernal craft projects. The house is littered with the fruits of her labors—the macramé owl she made back before I was even born, the hand-knitted afghans draped over every chair and couch. There are even a couple of those damn dolls left.

When I was about nine, Memaw got obsessed with making these rag dolls with little gingham dresses and yarn pigtails. The problem was, of course, that I never wanted to play with dolls.

I'd be playing with my Hot Wheels, and Memaw would keep making these dolls I never touched, until finally there were rag dolls sitting on every flat surface in the house, staring at me with blank, hand-stitched eyes. When I told her I was starting to have nightmares about the dolls, she loaded them all but her favorites into a big green garbage bag and gave them to the church toy drive.

After the dolls, the needlepoint Bible verses came—there's at least two in every room in the house, including the bathroom. Then came the animal shapes Uncle Bobby would cut out of plywood so Memaw could paint them. After she got tired of plywood geese and kittens, she started making refrigerator magnets out of bread dough. When those got old, she started in on the felt-and-sequin Christmas ornaments. She made so many we had to put up two trees just so we'd have room to hang them all.

Now it's eggs. Well, really they're egg dioramas. She's been on this kick for over a year. I think it's held her attention so long because it's both tedious and creative—and for a project to keep her interested, it has to be both of those things. The needlepoint Bible verses were just tedious; there's no creativity in copying words straight out of a book, even if it is the Good Book. The refrigerator magnets were kind of creative, but they were too easy to make—not tedious at all.

That's why the egg dioramas are perfect, as far as Memaw is concerned. They start out tedious. You use a pin to poke two tiny holes in the egg and stir up the yolk inside so it's all liquidy. Then you put your mouth over one of the tiny holes and blow the yolk out of the other.

After that you cut a little window in the hollow egg. This part is also tedious, because half the time the egg, which you've just spent 15 minutes cleaning out, shatters in your hand. I've asked Memaw why she doesn't cut the window in the egg first and just let the yolk fall out the window, but she says there's two ways of doing everything: the right way and the lazy way.

If you manage to cut the egg without breaking it, the creative part comes next—painting the egg inside and out, and after the paint dries, putting together a scene inside the egg, sticking a foam base in the egg's bottom, and gluing on the tiny figures that Memaw orders from a craft catalog.

Memaw's done all kinds of egg dioramas—nativity scenes with a tiny stable and Mary, Joseph, and baby Jesus; Easter scenes with little plastic bunnies and plastic eggs glued inside the real egg; even a crucifixion scene with a little bitty Jesus dying on a cross no bigger than a broken toothpick. I think the crucifixion one is kind of gross—who wants to look inside an egg and see a little plastic savior dying for the world's sins?—but Memaw says that one's her favorite.

Usually I get bored helping her with her projects, but tonight I don't mind. I'm still in a good mood from standing under the waterfall; from Bo and me, after all our months of driving, actually getting somewhere. As I put my lips over the hole in the egg, my mind starts wandering to places I tell it not to go. But my mind has a mind of its own, and I find myself closing my eyes and imagining that instead of pressing my lips to an egg, I'm really pressing my lips against Wendy's. I try to imagine to the softness of her little pink mouth and wonder what it would feel like to kiss and be kissed back.

"I ain't even gonna ask you what you're thinkin' about," Memaw says, touching my shoulder.

I jump, and my hand squeezes without me wanting it to. Slimy yolk runs down my wrist to my elbow. I wipe my arm clean with a paper towel and dump the shattered shell into the trash. With handling eggs and with liking Wendy, I decide, the same rule applies: Proceed with caution.

X X X

"Hey, H.F., how's it hangin'?" Marijane is sitting on the counter in the girls' bathroom, smoking a Marlboro red right under the sign that says NO SMOKING.

I look down at the front of my jeans. "Unless I'm missin' somethin', I don't think it's hangin' at all."

Marijane laughs and lets out a huge puff of smoke. Marijane or one of her friends is always sitting just inside the bathroom, breathing smoke like some dragon guarding the entrance to a cave full of treasure.

The thing is, I always like those girls. Memaw would kill me if I ever tried to go out of the house wearing what Marijane has on: sprayed-on jeans, a cut-off Harley-Davidson T-shirt that says BOLD AND FEARLESS, and long chain earrings that hang down to her shoulders. But I like her look. It says the same thing as that flag with the snake on it: *Don't tread on me.*

"Wanna cancer stick?" She flicks the back of the Marlboro pack so that one cigarette sticks out.

"No, thanks...just came in to pee before study hall."

I have to pee because I'm a nervous wreck. Wendy is in study hall with me, and I swore on that waterfall yesterday that I was gonna make myself talk to her. My bladder feels like it's gonna let go with the force of a waterfall, so I head for a stall.

"Say...H.F.," Marijane hollers, "you learn to piss standin' up yet?"

"Still practicin'," I say, as I unzip and squat.

It probably sounds like Marijane gives me a hard time about being the way I am—and she does—but I can't help liking her, because she's so good-natured about it. If she calls me a dyke, then she makes sure she calls herself a slut in the same breath, so that's fine with me. If Marijane is gonna say something about you, she says it to your face, not like the whispering snub queens on the cheerleading squad.

I think the real reason I like Marijane is because I wonder if she's like my mom was when she went to Morgan High. In that picture of her in her Van Halen T-shirt with her cigarette and her sneer, she don't look that different from Marijane. I'm not a thing like Marijane and her friends—I don't drink beer or smoke pot or run around with foul-mouthed boys—but those girls all seem to like me fine. I hope this means my mom would like me fine too.

As I'm leaving the bathroom, Marijane throws her cigarette butt into the sink with a hiss. "Hang in there, H.F.," she says. "Don't let them bastards get you down."

I walk into study hall, where Mr. McNeil is sitting at the teacher's desk, already deep into his Louis L'Amour novel. He never looks up the whole period, no matter how loud people get. I have a theory that he's got on earplugs like factory workers wear to protect their eardrums against the noisy machinery. That's the only way I figure that he could stand the racket.

I can't stand it half the time myself, and the idea that you're supposed to be studying while the paper wads whiz past your head and the football players have farting contests is the biggest joke in this joke of a school. You'd be better off trying to study in a monkey house.

I take a deep breath and start inching my way between rows so I can get the seat next to Wendy, but I'm stopped dead when Travis Rose, the captain of the football team, grabs my shirttail. "Hey, H.F.," he says, "where's your girlfriend?"

He means Bo. This, of course, is the football team's idea of some great humor. "Sorry," I say, "it's against my religion to answer stupid questions."

I look him dead in the eye, but he still won't let go of my shirt. He's having too good of a time, and his buddies are laughing like he's the funniest comedian on earth.

Travis grins. "Aw, you're just jealous 'cause you ain't got no flute for your little girlfriend to blow on."

Memaw says I get mad like my momma. I get real quiet, my spine turns to concrete, and my eyes feel like they shoot out heat rays like Superman's. When I finally do say something, my voice is quiet and even. "Now, Travis, what would I need a dick of my own for when I can stand here and talk to the biggest dick in the whole school?" I don't like to use foul language, but you've got to talk to people in a way they'll understand.

Travis's buddies sit there, waiting to see what he's gonna do, ready to play their usual game of follow the leader. Travis's face is red, and I can almost hear the squeaky wheels turning in his pitiful excuse for a brain.

He's mad enough to hit me, but the redneck code of honor says you don't hit a girl...at least not in public. If you're in private and she's your girlfriend, that's different. Finally, he lets go of my shirttail and mutters, "Fuckin' dyke."

After I'm safely past Travis and his cronies, I sneak a glance back at Mr. McNeil at his desk. He's lost in L'Amour Land, galloping through the sagebrush instead of supervising study hall.

One thing I'll say for Travis and his buddies, they've made me forget how nervous I was about talking to Wendy. I plop right down next to her without even thinking about it. She's wearing this yellow dress covered in tiny green leaves that makes her look like the trees I saw yesterday with the sun shining through them. She's reading a paperback with a cover that says *Nine Stories*, which, in my opinion, isn't much of a title in the attention-grabbing department. It sounds generic, like when you see those white cans in the grocery store that just say DOG FOOD in plain black letters.

Wendy mutters something under her breath that from where I'm sitting sounds like "fat souls."

"I beg your pardon?" I say.

She sets down her book and looks up, and all of a sudden I can see why people talk about redheads and tempers. "Assholes," she says. "Those guys are such assholes. If there's anything the slightest bit different about you, it's like it's their God-given duty to harass you. Like with you...just because you don't look like one of their cutesy-poo cheerleaders, they've got to give you a hard time. And with me and my red hair, they're always like, 'Hey, carrot top' this and 'Little Orphan Annie' that. I *hate* that. I mean, my God, it's only hair. How trivial can you be?" She sucks in her breath, then lets it out. "Assholes."

This is the most I've ever heard from Wendy. I think about Marijane in the bathroom. "Well, you know what they say. 'Don't let them bastards get you down.'"

Wendy's little pink mouth turns up at the corners. It feels good that she's smiling at something I said, even if I did just get it off Marijane.

"Good advice," Wendy says, "but it's kind of hard to follow day in and day out. When we lived in Scranton, I thought it sucked, but that was before I saw Morgan. I mean, I didn't even know towns like this existed."

"I guess you wouldn't...know towns like this existed, I mean." My nerves are coming back on me. All of a sudden, I can't stop thinking about Wendy being a college professor's daughter from up North. She's too good for this dried-up little coal-mining town, and since I can count on two hands the times I've been outside this town, that must mean she's too good for me.

"You know," Wendy says, "when Dad told me we were moving to a little town in Kentucky, I was dumb enough to think it would be easy to make friends here. I thought small towns were supposed to be friendly, and Southerners were supposed to be friendly, so I figured on my first day of school everybody would come up and ask me to...I don't know, eat fried chicken and biscuits on their front porch or something. And instead I get treated like a...like a..."

"Redheaded stepchild?" I hate myself as soon as I say it, but thank the lord, Wendy laughs.

She wraps a strand of fiery hair around her finger. "What is it with red hair anyway? Ever since I hit the Bible Belt, it's like red hair equals bride of Satan or something. Maybe I should dye it."

"No!" I almost shout. "Never do that. It's the most beautiful hair I've seen in my life." I shut my mouth, but it's too late. I feel my face heat up like it's gonna catch fire and burn down the school, like in that movie about that Holiness girl with ESP that I sneaked and watched one night after Memaw was asleep.

"Thank you," Wendy says. If she knows I'm embarrassed, she doesn't show it. "Nah, I'm not really going to dye it. It wouldn't make any difference anyway. I'd still be the daughter of one of those weirdos over at the college." She smiles and crinkles her nose. Cute.

"Well, uh..." I nod in the direction of that generic-looking book on her desk. "I'll let you get back to your book. I don't mean to keep pesterin' you."

"You're not a pest, H.F. It's nice to have somebody to talk to for a change. Some days I come home from school and realize I haven't said a word to anybody all day."

I think of the words on Marijane's T-shirt: BOLD AND FEARLESS. "Uh...well, there ain't no excuse for you to go all day by yourself like that. Like, when we're in the lunchroom, you don't have to sit at a table by yourself and read a book." I have to swallow hard before the next words come out. "You could sit with Bo and me."

She smiles like I just made her an offer to do something much more appealing than sit at what gets called the "freak table." "Well, H.F.," she says, "I think I'm going to have to take you up on that."

I can't believe how easy this is. The girl must be plain starved for friendliness. "Well, you know, it ain't fried chicken and biscuits on the front porch, but maybe we could set that up sometime too. My memaw makes biscuits so fluffy it's like bitin' into a cloud. So...so...maybe you could come over for supper some evenin'. We never eat on the front porch before, but hey, if that's what you think we're supposed to do down here, we could give it a try."

Shut up, H.F., I'm telling myself even as I talk. You don't want this college professor's daughter over at your tacky little house, picking at her pinto beans and staring slack-jawed at all the egg dioramas. But the words keep spilling out, and when I finally stop them and look at Wendy, she's still grinning.

When the bell rings, I swagger out of study hall, as proud as one of the cowboys in the book Mr. McNeil has never even looked up from reading.

FOUR

It's official. Wendy and me are friends. Well, Wendy and Bo and me. Since that day in study hall, we've been as tight as the Three Musketeers, the Three Little Pigs, and the Father, Son, and Holy Ghost, although Memaw would probably say I was blaspheming if she heard that.

Every pretty day after school, except on Mondays when Wendy has her piano lesson, we've done the same thing we're doing right now: sit around Deer Creek, right next to the waterfall. Usually me and Wendy take off our shoes and wade in the creek. Bo still won't get his feet wet, but he's taken to bringing his flute with him. While me and Wendy splash around in the water, he'll sit on a rock and play. The music floats up to the tops of the trees, and the birds chirp right along, probably trying to figure out what strange kind of bird is singing such a long and complicated song. Wendy is holding her skirt up over her knees while she does a splashing dance in the creek. Her legs are china-doll white. "You know, all the bullshit we go through in school is just about worth it for this," she says, her hair glinting in the sunshine.

She's right. Here by the waterfall, Wendy and Bo and me make up our own world. I know nature can be just as nasty as high school, what with big animals eating little animals and strong critters beating up on weak critters. But here at Deer Creek you'd never think nature was anything but peaceful—a place where everybody, no matter how small or weak or different, can be safe from harm.

Bo sets down his flute. "You know, I've never been what

you'd call an outdoor type of person. Nature's just always meant bugs and dirt to me. But this place is different."

"It's like *The Secret Garden*," Wendy says. "God, when I was about ten years old I carried that book around like a Bible. Have you read it?"

Bo and me shake our heads, which shouldn't surprise Wendy by now. She's always going on about books Bo and me have never read. The only books I read when I was ten were the Hardy Boys and Nancy Drew. I tried the Bobbsey Twins once, but they were so goody-goody I wanted to smack 'em.

"It's about a little orphan girl," Wendy says. "She finds this garden that's been locked up for years, and it totally transforms her life."

"Well, I reckon some people like gardenin' a whole lot," I say. I help Memaw put out tomatoes every year, but except for the produce, I can't quite see how having a garden would transform your life.

"It's also kind of like Never-Never Land in *Peter Pan*," Wendy says, trying for a story us illiterate hicks might have heard of.

"Well, your name is Wendy," I say. I may not have read *The Secret Garden* or anything by that J.D. what's-his-name she's always talking about, but by God, I have seen some Disney cartoons.

"Don't go lookin' at me to be no Peter Pan," Bo says, stretching out on his rock. "I get in enough trouble without prancin' around in a pair of green tights."

Wendy smiles. "H.F. can be Peter Pan."

I blush because I'm thinking, wasn't Wendy, like, Peter Pan's love interest? "But Peter Pan's a boy," I say.

"Yeah," Wendy says, "but when I was little Mom and Dad took me to see the play *Peter Pan* in Philadelphia. A girl played him—this little muscular girl with short hair. I can still see her flying over the stage. Come to think of it, she kind of looked like you."

Now I'm blushing to the roots of my hair, and the cat's run away with my tongue again. "So," Bo says, filling in the silence, "if you're Wendy and H.F. is Peter Pan, who am I supposed to be?"

"John or Michael," Wendy says. "Take your pick."

Bo grins. "At least you didn't say Tinkerbell."

✗ ✗ ✗

When Bo is about to drop Wendy off in front of her house, Wendy says, "So, H.F., do you want to come spend the night Friday? Mom's been pestering me about having friends over." Wendy gives Bo a squeeze on the shoulder. "I'd invite you too, General Beauregard, but my dad wouldn't take very kindly to a boy sleeping over."

"Even if we was just to giggle and paint each other's toe-nails?"

Wendy laughs. "Even if." She looks me right in the eye, which turns my stomach into gooey apple butter. "So, H.F., what do you say?"

"Um...sure. I mean, I've got to ask Memaw and everything, but I'm pretty sure it'll be all right."

"Great! See ya." Wendy half-runs to her front door. It's a nice house—all brick, probably with at least three bedrooms. Probably not a scrap of cheap paneling or an egg diorama in the whole place.

"So," Bo says as he drives us back toward town, "I reckon you're feelin' pretty good about yourself, huh?"

"I don't know. I mean, I looked at that fancy house of hers, and all I could think was, what would I say to somebody who lives in a house like that?"

"Wendy lives in that house, and you talk to her all the time...when you don't get tongue-tied, that is."

"But what about her parents? Her daddy's a professor, and her momma's all educated too. I don't know how to act in front of people like that. I don't know which fork to use at supper...or...or how to hold my teacup right. They're gonna think I'm ignorant, Bo. And you know what? They're gonna be right."

"Lord God, H.F. There's just no pleasin' you, is there? You get your panties all in a wad about wantin' this girl to like you back, and when she finally does, you start pissin' and moanin' about meetin' her parents."

"Well, first of all, Bo, she don't like me back that way. She just wants a girl for a friend, and in this pitiful excuse for a town, I'm the best she can do."

When Bo takes his eyes off the road to look at me, I'm surprised how sad he looks. "Well," he sighs, "even if Wendy don't like you that way, you and her are still gettin' awful close, and before long you're gonna be wantin' to get rid of your third wheel."

We're parked in front of my house, and Bo looks close to tears. "But Bo, me and Wendy need a third wheel. You know why?"

"Why?"

"Because you and me and Wendy—we're a tricycle."

Bo smiles a little. "But what if you decide you're happier bein' a bicycle?"

"Now, Bo, you know just as well as I do that you can't just take a wheel off a tricycle and call it a bicycle; the danged thing'd fall right over. Look, no matter what happens with Wendy and me, I'm not gonna leave you by the wayside."

"You'd better not, H.F., 'cause if you do, you'll be leavin' me with nobody but a bunch of rednecks who'll beat the livin' daylights out of me."

I grab Bo's hand and hold it. It's long-fingered, fine-boned—a musician's hand. "Don't worry," I grin. "I don't never forget my friends. How could I? I've only got two of 'em."

Bo sniffs a little. I've seen him do this at the movies before, when he's trying not to cry. "Well, speakin' of gettin' the livin' daylights beat out of me, I'd better get on home before Daddy decides to take his belt off. And sugar, you'd better go on in that house and ask your memaw about stayin' all night at Wendy's."

✗ ✗ ✗

Memaw's frying salmon patties, and you can smell them all over the house. If I cracked a window, every cat in the neighborhood would be in our yard. I hear the oil sputtering in her cast iron skillet.

Memaw likes to sing hymns while she cooks. Right now, it's "Bringing in the Sheaves." The woman is a walking hymnal—if a song has anything to do with God or Jesus, chances are, she knows it. Right now, hearing her plain, clear voice singing about bringing in the sheaves, and smelling the fishy smell, I think about that Bible story with the loaves and the fishes—about how Jesus made a little bit of food turn into enough for a whole bunch of people.

I don't have faith the size of a mustard seed or even the size of one of those critters you have to look in a microscope to see. But right now I like thinking about that Bible story. I may not have much in my life, but I've got Bo and Wendy's friendship. I've got Wendy wanting me to stay all night on Friday, and I've got Memaw cooking in the kitchen. That might not be a lot, but right now that little bit seems like enough.

Like always, I wish I had my momma too, but even without her, I feel pretty happy.

"Hey, Memaw," I say as I walk into the kitchen. She's lifting the patties out of the pan and setting them on a paper towel to soak up the grease.

"Well, Faith, you sure are pussyfootin' around this evenin'. I didn't even hear you come in."

"I'm just sneaky, I guess." I start getting out the glasses and silverware without even being asked. I don't think Memaw's gonna say no when I ask her if I can stay over at Wendy's, but I want to get on her good side just in case.

"Oh, you're about as sneaky as a freight train," she says, dishing up a plate of salmon, macaroni and cheese, and cream-style corn. "You've never been able to hide anything from me to save your life. It's just like that little china cat with the broke ear."

I shovel in a mouthful of macaroni. The one-eared china cat still sits on one of the umpteen dozen knickknack shelves in the living room. Memaw's told the story about it a thousand times—sometimes to me, sometimes to other old people to illustrate my good character: "I reckon you was about three years old, and you just fell in love with this little china cat your uncle Bobby brung me as a souvenir from one place or the other. I said you could look at the kitty, but not to touch it because if it got broke, you could cut yourself on it. I wasn't worried about the cat bein' valuable, you understand; I was worried about you. Children are what's valuable on this earth. I like havin' all my pretty things around me, but they ain't worth a plugged nickel when you compare 'em to people." Memaw likes this story. I can tell because she's so wrapped up in it she's forgotten to stop talking every once in a while to eat.

"Of course," she says, "one day I got busy doin' somethin'—I think it was about the time I was makin' them crocheted covers for the Kleenex boxes—and I left you in the livin' room lookin' at Mister Rogers. Well, sir, I reckon that little china cat just started callin' out to you to come play with it. The next thing I knowed, you come toddlin' into the kitchen with tears the size of dimes rollin' down your face. You had the little china cat in one hand and its ear in the other. You just looked up at me with them big blue eyes and said, 'Memaw, I bwoked it.' Well, of course, I had to hug your neck on accounta you bein' so honest. Most kids—your mother included—woulda hid that little cat and hoped I'd never notice it was missin'. But not you—there ain't a sneaky bone in your body." She finally cuts off a piece of salmon patty and eats it.

I know Memaw will say yes when I ask her about staying all night with Wendy. Whether she's got a right to or not, she trusts me. "Memaw," I say, "Wendy Cook asked me to stay all night at her house Friday. Is that all right?"

"Cook...Cook..." She chews thoughtfully. "Now, who's her people?"

"She's from up in Pennsylvania. Her daddy teaches over at the college. I think her mom's got some kind of job at the college too."

"Teachers, huh? I reckon that's all right, then. But I'll get awful lonesome rattlin' around in this old house all by myself."

I swallow hard. "I don't have to go if you don't want me to."

"Oh, of course I want you to go, Faith. Some of the best times I ever had growin' up was when I'd stay all night with one of my little girlfriends. Everybody else in the house'd be asleep, but we'd just lay awake in bed together and talk and giggle about the craziest things."

In bed together? I've already been a nervous wreck about

what to say to Wendy's family, but I hadn't given any thought to the sleeping arrangements. Thinking about crawling into the same bed with Wendy is like thinking about skydiving out of an airplane: exciting and terrifying at the same time. I try to imagine laying beside her, seeing her flaming hair spread out on a pillow, and all of a sudden, I feel like I'm gonna pass out.

"Faith, are you all right, honey?"

I nod feebly and push away my plate. For the first time in my life, I don't go back for more of Memaw's macaroni and cheese.

FIVE

I've been a nervous wreck all day. In world history, Mr. Clayton called on me, and I jumped like a bullet flew past my head. Everybody laughed, except Mr. Clayton.

That's something I've been trying to comfort myself thinking—that real adults don't tend to laugh at you the way other kids do. That's not to say grown-ups don't look at you like you're some three-headed alien that just landed on this planet, but for the most part they don't bust out laughing.

I hope Wendy's parents don't laugh at me and don't look at me like I'm something out of a science fiction movie. To tell the truth, I want them to love me. I want them to think I'm witty and charming and sophisticated, even though I'm not any of those, especially sophisticated. Good Lord, except for that one time Bobby drove Memaw and me to Lexington to the eye doctor and after that we ate at Frisch's, the only restaurants I've ever been in are Hardee's and the Dixie Diner. I guess girls that get raised by little old ladies don't get out much.

As soon as Wendy gets out of band practice, Bo's gonna drive me to her house. I'm pacing back and forth in the hall so hard I'm probably wearing a path in the floor. Isn't it weird how you can spend all this time wishing for something, and then when it looks like you're actually gonna get it, all you can think about is whether you need to go pee or throw up?

When the band room door swings open, Wendy and Bo are the first ones out. "Hey, H.F.," Wendy says, smiling. "Where's your overnight bag?"

"I've got all my stuff in here." I point to my schoolbag. It says something for how often Memaw gets out that there's not a single piece of luggage in the house. When I asked her about it, she said, "There used to be an old Samsonite suit satchel, but your mother took it when she left, and I reckon I just never got around to buyin' another un."

It was Bo's idea for me to put my things in my schoolbag, which is a lot less humiliating than carrying them in a paper sack like I'd thought about doing. The stuff fits in with my books fine, since all I packed was a shirt to sleep in, a toothbrush, a clean T-shirt, and a change of drawers.

Bo's been great about getting me ready to stay at Wendy's. He even went to the library and got me a copy of Emily Post's book on manners, so I could study it. No matter how many forks the Cooks have at their supper table, I'm ready for them.

I'm so quiet in the car, listening to the butterflies flap around in my stomach, that Bo leans over and whispers, "Relax, H.F. Lord, you'd think I was drivin' you to the women's penitentiary."

I make myself take a deep breath and feel so much better that I realize I must've been forgetting to breathe. I wonder if you could die that way. I can see the doctors leaning over my corpse saying, "Well, it looks like this girl got herself in such a tizzy she done forgot to breathe."

I come back down to earth when the car stops and I hear Wendy say, "Thanks, Bo. I wish you could stay with us too."

"Well," Bo says, "I wouldn't want your daddy comin' after me with a shotgun."

Wendy laughs. "You wouldn't have to worry about that. Dad isn't the shotgun type. He'd be more likely to back you into a corner and drill you on grammar."

"Lord, that'd be even worse," Bo says.

We just sit there a few seconds until Bo says, "H.F., was

you plannin' on gettin' out of the car any time soon?"

"Oh...sorry." I'd forgotten I was sitting in the front seat of a two-door car. I have to get out of the front before Wendy can get out of the back. God, how can I make Wendy's parents think I'm witty and charming when I can't even remember to do things like breathe and get out of a car?

"Bye, girls. Remember to have fun, H.F." Bo drives away, leaving us standing in front of Wendy's well-kept brick house. Memaw always thinks of brick homes as the big sign that a person's making good in the world. She says my papaw always wanted to make enough money to buy them a brick home, but it wasn't the Lord's will. "I reckon," she always says, "some of us was just meant to have our riches up in heaven." I always wonder if she thinks that when she passes through the pearly gates, St. Peter's gonna give her a gold key that opens the door to her own three-bedroom brick ranch-style house, filled up with enough craft projects to last her an eternity.

"Come on in, H.F." Wendy's voice makes me remember that I'm not standing outside Memaw's house in heaven, but Wendy's neighborhood is the closest thing Morgan has to a subdivision.

In the living room there's nothing but books, books, books. The walls are lined with shelves that look like they could fall over from the weight of the books that are wedged and stacked in them. More books are stacked up on the floor next to the bookshelves, like they're waiting in line in case any shelf space opens up. There's some furniture in the room—a green couch and chair—but mostly it looks like the reason the Cooks need a roof over their heads is so their books won't get wet.

"You got more books in here than the Morgan Public Library," I say.

"Not that that's saying much," Wendy says back, reminding

me how tiny my world is. The only library I've spent much time in is the one at school. The only time I go to Morgan Public—which always seems big to me—is when Billy Graham has a new book out and I go get it for Memaw.

"I thought I heard somebody. Hi, you two." When I turn to face the voice, I see that Wendy's hair color doesn't come from her mother, but her taste in clothes does. Mrs. Cook's shoulder-length hair is as mouse-brown as mine, except for a few gray streaks, but she's wearing a light-purple, flowered skirt that I'm pretty sure I've seen Wendy wear before. The gray in Mrs. Cook's hair and the lines on her face make her look older than most mothers of girls our age.

"Mom, this is H.F. H.F., this is Mom."

I can see a little bit of Wendy in Mrs. Cook's smile. "It's a pleasure to meet you, Mrs. Cook, ma'am."

"Oh, you can drop that formal stuff," Wendy's mom laughs. "It makes me sound old enough to be a Confederate widow. Just call me Carolyn." She sips from a glass I've just noticed for the first time.

"Carolyn," I say, but I'm having a hard time acting normal, because I know the golden liquid in Wendy's mom's glass is not Coca-Cola. Memaw says drinking alcohol is willful sinning, and while I don't know if anything you do is sinful as long as you're just doing it to yourself, I can't get used to seeing somebody drinking out in the open, without acting ashamed or worried about what somebody might think.

"Can I get you girls something to drink?" Carolyn says, and I say "No, thank you" too quick, even though I don't honestly think she's offering liquor to a couple of 16-year-olds.

"Well, then, I guess I'll go out and water the flowers," she says. "Make yourself at home, H.F. Help yourself to a snack if you get hungry. We won't start dinner until the powers that be at Randall College see fit to unshackle Wendy's dad from his desk in the English department." Barefoot, Carolyn walks out the front door, with her watering can in one hand and her drink in the other.

Wendy and I stand in the living room and look at each other for a second, then we both smile at the same time. "So...uh," Wendy says, "I guess I could give you the grand tour, if you'd like."

"Sure."

I follow her out of the living room and into the dining room, which makes me review all of Emily's silverware rules in my mind. The kitchen even has bookshelves full of books called things like *An Introduction to Indian Cooking* and *The French Chef*. I wonder if the French book has recipes for frogs and snails, but I decide not to ask. And I wouldn't even know what would be in an Indian cookbook, except maybe recipes for corn and buffalo.

There's a piano in the den and a stereo and lots of shelves of CDs. But the funny thing is, there's no TV...not in the living room, not in the den, nowhere I can see. "Y'all don't have a TV?" My brain's been full of questions since I walked into the house, but this is the first one that's made it out of my mouth.

"Nope," Wendy smiles. "We're one of those weird families that likes to sit around and talk."

"Huh." I've never thought about people not having a TV not because they were too poor to buy one, but because they just plain didn't want one.

I follow Wendy down the hall, past the bathroom, past another room full of books that she calls "the study," which I think is a weird thing to call a room. She leads me into the next door on the right and says, "My room."

When I first walk through the beaded curtain, I feel like I'm gonna pass out. I'm so surrounded by Wendy—by her, by her things, by a feeling I can only call "Wendyness"—that I'm afraid my knees are about to buckle.

The walls are painted peach—the same peachy color that shines through her skin. The bed is piled with big pillows covered with all kinds of crazy patterns, and a white net canopy hangs over the whole thing. A rainbow-colored poster on the wall says LOVE in big squiggly letters, like it's a sign advertising how I feel.

Wendy flops down on the bed and props herself up on a purple pillow. She pats the pillow beside her. "Come on," she says, "make yourself comfortable."

"Uh...I think I'll just stand for a minute." I walk over to her bookshelf and try to act like I'm interested in what's on it, but the titles swim in front of my eyes, like all those red-and-white Campbell's Soup cans in the grocery store.

I'm getting dizzy staring at the books, so I walk over to her dresser. But looking at that stuff's even worse...thinking about the hairbrush sliding through her thick halo of hair, the talcum powder she dusts all over her body with that fuzzy pink powder puff. When I look up to escape all her personal things, I face myself in the mirror and see how hard I'm blushing.

It seems like I've had three birthdays since anybody said anything, so I nod toward the purple, green, and gold beads that are hanging down over the mirror and say, "Nice beads."

"I got those last year at Mardi Gras."

"Cool," I say, trying not to give away too much of my ignorance. All I know about Mardi Gras is that it's one more reason Memaw thinks the Catholics are gonna burn in hell.

"H.F., are you sure you don't want to sit down?"

I sit on the straight-backed wooden chair in front of Wendy's desk. It's not that comfortable, but there's no way I'm gonna get on the bed with her now, especially not with her momma roaming around the house all liquored up. "I like your room," I say finally. "Everything in it looks just like you."

Wendy smiles. "Well, maybe you can show me your room sometime."

"There ain't much to it. Not like this. I've just got me a little single bed and a chest of drawers shoved up against the wall in the little room where Memaw keeps her sewin' machine. When my mother had me, Memaw turned half of her sewin' room into a nursery with a little crib and changin' table. It seems like Memaw would've moved me into Momma's old room after she left, but instead she just kept me in my little corner of the sewin' room, and when I outgrew my crib, she sold it off and moved in the bed I sleep in now and replaced the changin' table with the chest of drawers. She kept my mom's room just the same. Maybe she thought if she left it just the way it was, she would come back to it someday. Or maybe she was afraid that if I moved into Momma's old room, I'd take a notion to leave too." Great, I think. First I couldn't think of nothing to say. Now you can't shut me up.

But Wendy seems interested. "Does your grandmother talk much about your mom?" You can tell Wendy ain't from around here, because she can't quite wrap her mouth around words like "Memaw." If she says something about her grandmother, she calls her "Gramma," just like she was saying "grammar" but without the "r" on the end.

"Sometimes she'll tell a story about when Mom was little, but she don't like to talk about the time around when she left."

"I guess not. You said your mom was 16 when she had you?"

"She turned 16 right after I was born."

"God, H.F., can you imagine getting pregnant at the age we are now?"

I say I can't, but the truth is, I can't imagine myself getting pregnant at any age.

Wendy hugs her knees to her chest. "I mean, when you're 16, it's like the whole world's out there waiting for you, but then if you get pregnant, the world shrinks to the size of the baby in your belly. All of a sudden you have to worry about taking care of someone else's needs before you've even learned what your own are. I don't know...I think if I found myself in that situation, I'd have an abortion."

"But Momma would've had to figure out how to get all the way to Lexington or Knoxville to get one, and Memaw would've killed her dead if she found out. Plus," I say, "then there wouldn't have been a me."

Wendy smiles. "Well, I'm glad there is a you. You and Bo have been the only people at Morgan High who haven't treated me like, what was it you said? A redheaded godchild?"

"Stepchild," I laugh. "A redheaded stepchild."

✗ ✗ ✗

When Wendy's dad comes home, he gets to work grilling hamburgers in the backyard. The Cooks eat supper at 7 o'clock, which is two whole hours later than me and Memaw usually eat.

As it turns out, Wendy's red hair comes from her dad. The top of his head is slick, bald, and pink like a baby's butt with a diaper rash, but the fringe of hair that grows around the sides of his head is bright orange. If he wasn't so serious, he'd put you in mind of a clown.

All that memorizing from Emily Post turned out to be a waste of time because all we have for supper is hamburgers and french fries. Ain't a fork in sight. The food is good. Memaw's great at making beans and corn bread and macaroni and cheese, but when she makes hamburgers and french fries, which she don't do often, she just fries the patties in a skillet and fixes frozen french fries that come in a bag. Mrs. Cook's fries are homemade from real potatoes.

Wendy and me get Coke to drink, but Mr. and Mrs. Cook are drinking beer right out of the bottle. Memaw would die.

"So, H.F.," Mr. Cook says, "have you always lived in Morgan?"

Wendy has already told me her dad asks lots of questions. She says he don't mean nothing by it but that sometimes a conversation with him feels like you're facing that Spanish Inquisition we read about in world history class.

"Yessir," I say. "My whole family's from Morgan or thereabouts. Memaw was raised in the Argon coal camp. It was a few miles south of Morgan, close to the Tennessee state line. Some of the houses from the camp's still standing if you was ever to want to see 'em."

Before I know what I'm doing, I'm rattling off Memaw's life story—how she grew up in the coal camp and met my papaw when she was 17 years old, how Papaw didn't want to be a coal miner and so he and Memaw moved to town after they got married and he took a job in the hardware store, where he worked till he went off to fight in World War II and got part of his leg blowed off. I talk and talk and talk, and you'd think Mr. Cook would be bored out of his mind, but instead he looks so interested that I wouldn't be surprised if he whipped out a writing pad and started taking notes.

"Fascinating," he says, and even though I know he means it in a good way, I still feel like a bug under a microscope.

"I think it's great that you have your family so close at hand," Mrs. Cook says, and I wonder if Wendy has told her about my mother taking off. "Sometimes I wonder," she says, "if people are making a mistake when they move all the way across the country to take jobs and so forth. Of course, I guess it's more of an economic necessity than a choice."

Mrs. Cook drinks some more beer, and I wonder if she, like Wendy, is less than happy about their move to Kentucky. Maybe I should change the subject. "So, Mrs...I mean, Carolyn, what do you do over at the college?"

She rolls her eyes. "Less than I'd like, to be honest. When they gave Stan the job in the English department, they said I could be the curator of the Randall College art gallery. I was really excited at the time."

"Mom was the assistant curator of a gallery in Scranton," Wendy says.

"Right," Carolyn continues, "and so I was excited to be moving up from assistant curator to curator. Little did I know that the Randall College art gallery was one dusty room with the same paintings hanging in it since 1977. The same *lousy* paintings, I might add. So it's a made-up, part-time job basically, but I'm trying to make the best of it. I'm thinking about putting together some shows by local artists. Wendy says the art teacher at the high school does some interesting work. You wouldn't happen to know any good local artists, would you?"

I think of Memaw's bread-dough refrigerator magnets and egg dioramas. "No," I say.

After we eat, we sit in the den. Carolyn asks Wendy to play something on the piano. Wendy rolls her eyes but sits down at the bench anyway. I've heard the plink-plink-plinky piano playing when Memaw makes me go to church, but the way Wendy plays is different. Her hands move all over the keyboard, hitting so many notes at the same time that it's hard to believe all that music is coming from one little piano.

And then there's the way she looks. I try not to stare at her too hard while she plays, because I'm afraid her parents will see how I'm looking at her. To try to keep from staring at Wendy, I look at the picture that's hanging above the piano. It's a fuzzy-looking painting of a redheaded girl in old-fashioned clothes playing the piano. Except for the old-fashioned clothes, she looks just like Wendy.

When Wendy finishes, her mom and dad clap, so I do too. "Thanks for playing the Bach, honey. You know it's my favorite," Carolyn says.

Then Mr. Cook sets down his beer bottle and takes a guitar out of its case. "So, H.F.," he starts, and I'm terrified he's gonna try to make me sing or something, "how about a little C, S, N, and Y?"

"Sure," I say, even though I have no idea what he's talking about, and he might as well be saying, "So, H.F., how about we cook you up and eat you?"

But instead he starts strumming the guitar and singing some song about teaching your children well. Carolyn joins in, and they sound real good together.

When they finish, I clap, and Wendy says, "So, H.F., now you know the truth. My parents are a pair of overeducated hippies."

"Well," I say, "I reckon that's all right." I've heard Memaw talk about hippies, about the long-haired do-gooders that came to Kentucky around the time my mother was little. Memaw says they all talked about wanting to save the Appalachian mountains and the Appalachian people, but she could never figure out what they were trying to save the Appalachian people from. And besides, she always says, she don't need no stringy-headed college boy from up North trying to save her; she's done been saved by Jesus.

Mr. Cook goes into the kitchen and comes back with two

more bottles of beer. "Well, Carolyn," he says, "do you think the old folks should clear out of the way and leave these girls to their own devices?"

Carolyn takes one of the beers and opens it. "I suppose they've had all they want of us old fogeys. See you in the morning, girls. And I know you'll be up till all hours, but do try to get some sleep tonight."

I gulp as I picture Wendy's big bed and wonder where—and if—I'm gonna sleep tonight.

Six

Wendy's stretched out on the bed, propped up on her purple pillow. She changed into her nightgown in the bathroom, which I was halfway glad of. Sometimes, like in the locker room at P.E., when girls take their clothes off like it's nothing just because they're in front of other girls, I get so embarrassed I have to stick my head in a locker so I can't see them and they can't see me.

Don't get me wrong. I would've liked to see Wendy with no clothes on. I just feel like looking at her would've turned me to stone, like the men who looked at that Medusa we read about one time in junior high.

"Mom and Dad really like you. I can tell," Wendy says. She's stretched out and relaxed in her white nightgown, like a long white cat. And me, I've finally brought myself to sit down on the bed, but I'm sitting at the foot—so close to the edge that half my butt is hanging off.

"That's good. I kept worryin' I'd say somethin' that'd give away how ignorant I am."

Wendy picks up a pillow and hits me with it. "H.F., you're not ignorant. You shouldn't put yourself down like that. You've got—what was it Dad said when I went in to say good night to him?—'a keen native intelligence.'"

I wonder what "native intelligence" means. The "native" part makes me think of cannibals with bones in their noses. "Well, that's good, I guess."

"You shouldn't worry about what my parents think. They're pretty laid back. You know, what I said about them being hippies is really true." Grinning, she leans down and picks up a photo album from the bottom shelf of her nightstand. "I've got to show you this picture of them in the '70s."

She flips open the book, and there's a snapshot of Mr. and Mrs. Cook, probably before they were married and way before there was a Wendy. Carolyn's mouse-brown hair is long and stringy past her shoulders, and she's wearing a flowered top and all these beads around her neck. But Mr. Cook's the real funny-looking one. Even though in the picture he's probably not much older than I am now, he's mostly bald on top. But the bright red hair on the sides of his head is long enough to touch his shoulders. He's got a mustache too, a long one that goes down to both sides of his chin, and he's wearing this fringy dress that looks like something an Indian might wear. Both Mr. and Mrs. Cook are wearing these teeny little round glasses that don't look hardly as big as their eyeballs.

"Pretty wild, huh?" Wendy says. "I like to keep this picture in case Mom and Dad drag out my baby pictures to show people. That way, I'm armed against embarrassment."

Below the photo of Mr. and Mrs. Cook is a picture of Wendy in pearls and a long black dress. She looks beautiful. She must see me looking at it, because she says, "That's from a couple of years ago—my piano recital in Scranton. Most of the other pictures are of my friends back in Pennsylvania."

I flip through the pictures of high school kids who all look like they can afford to go to the mall and buy new clothes anytime they feel like it. I flip through pretty fast until I come to a picture of Wendy, standing cheek-to-cheek next to this blond boy, who I think is a girl at first because he has smooth skin and hair down to his shoulders. He's touching Wendy, so unless he's related to her, I hate him. "Who's this?" I try to sound casual.

"That's Josh, my boyfriend back in Scranton."

I feel stupid for feeling hurt. Of course Wendy would have a boyfriend. In any town but Morgan, boys would be beating her door down to date her. And of course she likes boys. Most girls do. "Uh...is he still your boyfriend?"

Wendy shrugs. "Yes and no. We E-mail each other just about every day, so we're still close. But when I moved I told him it was unrealistic for us not to agree to see other people. So I'm sure he's dating around. And of course, I'm here in Morgan, where nobody has the slightest interest in me."

How can you not know? For a second, I'm scared I really said it instead of just thinking it, but Wendy keeps flipping through the album like nothing's wrong, so I guess I didn't say anything.

On the last page is another picture of Wendy's parents—this time looking the way they do now. They're at some kind of party where they're dressed up. Mr. Cook has a tie on, and Carolyn's wearing the same pearls Wendy had on in that other picture. They're holding glasses of wine and smiling.

I have to change the subject away from Wendy and boys, so without even thinking, I say, "Has your mother and daddy always drunk?"

"Huh?" Wendy says. "*Oh.* You mean, like, drinking alcohol, don't you?" She closes the album. "Hmm...I've never really thought about it, to tell you the truth, but yeah, I guess they're what you'd call moderate drinkers. They usually have a drink in the evening, maybe a few beers on Friday night. Why do you ask?"

"I don't know. Memaw's a pretty hard-shell Baptist, so I guess them drinkin' out in the open like that just seems...I don't know, like they might have a problem or something."

Wendy laughs, and I feel myself starting to shut her out. "Trust me, H.F., more often than not, the people who drink out in the open aren't the ones with problems. It's the people who try to keep their drinking hidden that you have to watch out for." Wendy sits up and hugs her knees to her chest. Her toenails are painted the same color as the inside of the big seashell Uncle Bobby brought Memaw back from Florida.

"When we first moved here," Wendy says, "Mom and Dad couldn't believe how provincial people were about alcohol. When somebody told Mom that Morgan was in a dry county, she thought that meant it didn't get much rain. She couldn't believe you actually had to drive across the state line to buy a six-pack."

"Huh. I guess Memaw always told me all drinkin' was bad, and I believed her without thinkin' much about it. Of course, I have thought about Bo's daddy. He gets drunk on payday and comes home and breaks dishes and calls Bo a faggot—"

"Well, Bo's dad is obviously an asshole, and drinking makes him even more of one."

What Wendy's saying makes sense. Memaw's always told me that drinking so much as one beer is like walking up to a booth and saying, "One ticket straight to hell, please." But from what I've seen of Wendy's parents, they're nice folks. If there is a God, it'd be awful small-minded of him to make them burn in hell on account of splitting a six-pack.

I've always known Memaw wouldn't understand about me liking girls, but the more I think about it, the more I realize that's not the only thing she doesn't understand. Memaw is the best-hearted person in the world, but sometimes I think she's too busy thinking about the next life to notice much of what's going on in this one.

"I bet you've never had a taste of alcohol in your life, have you, H.F.?"

"No. Have you?"

Wendy turns over on her side and stretches, fanning out her

little toes. "Sure. I've had a glass of wine at Christmas dinner ever since I was 12. That's how they do it in Europe. The idea is that if kids get exposed to small amounts of alcohol when they're young, it won't be a big deal to them when they're older. Dad says that America's Puritan heritage really shows in the popular attitude toward alcohol."

"Is that so?" I say, even though she's lost me on that part.

Suddenly Wendy hops up off the bed. "I'll be right back, OK?"

"OK." When she's safely out of the room, I pick up the pillow she's been laying on and smell it. It's like laying down in a flower garden. No matter how nice that boyfriend of hers up North is, I hate him with a purple passion.

I figured Wendy had just gone off to the bathroom, but when she comes back she's carrying two long-stemmed glasses filled a little over halfway with something deep purple. She closes the door behind her with her foot. "I'm about to corrupt you, H.F.," she says.

I feel tingly all over, but I try to act reasonable. "Wouldn't your mother and daddy be mad if they knew you was sneakin' liquor into your room?"

Wendy laughs. "It's not liquor—it's wine. And I'm not sneaking. Mom was in the kitchen, and I asked her very politely if we could each have half a glass of wine. She said yes, as long as a half a glass was all we had, and as long as your grandmother wouldn't mind. I kind of bent the truth a little and said she wouldn't." Wendy crinkles her nose.

Memaw would say she's leading me to temptation, and she may be, but damn, it feels good. I'd rather be led into temptation by Wendy Cook on earth than have a brick ranch-style house in heaven any day.

Wendy hands me the elegant, long-stemmed glass and sits

next to me on the bed. She sips from her own glass, then nods toward mine. "Try it," she says. And just like Adam in the Garden of Eden, I do what the pretty lady tells me.

The first sip is kind of sour, like grape juice that's been sitting out too long, which when you think about it, is what wine really is.

"You're supposed to hold it in your mouth a few seconds," Wendy says, "so you can taste the different flavors."

I swish the second sip around like mouthwash, and I'm surprised that there really are all kinds of different flavors in this little mouthful of wine. There's the sour part, which is all I tasted at first. But then there's also this peppery taste, and underneath that it's smooth, like vanilla.

"Like it?" Wendy asks.

"It's nice." I take another mouthful. "Now I understand that Bible story."

"What Bible story?"

"The one about the big wedding where they run out of wine, so Jesus turns the water into wine. That was a helluva party trick, wasn't it?"

Wendy laughs. "I guess so."

"Of course, Memaw always says that in Jesus' day they called grape juice wine, but that don't make no sense, does it? A bunch of grown-ups gettin' all excited about drinkin' plain ol' grape juice."

Wendy laughs again. Her laughter and the wine make me warm. "So, H.F., do you really believe in all that Bible stuff?"

"I don't guess so. Not any more than I believe in any other story. It's just that Memaw has filled my brain full of Bible stories from the time I was a little bitty girl, so they're always rattlin' around in there."

Wendy smiles and says, "Hmm."

"Hmm what?"

"Hmm nothing, really. I just like the way you talk."

"What's that supposed to mean?" I know I don't talk good English like the Cooks. Shoot, even the English teachers at school don't talk good English like the Cooks.

"The way you talk is like music. The expressions you use, the stories you tell. That's what you are, H.F.—a storyteller."

I like that. I like it a lot, to tell the truth. I take another sip of wine and notice that Wendy's setting down her empty glass on the nightstand. For all her talk about how you're supposed to slosh wine around in your mouth to taste it, she's gotten rid of hers pretty fast.

She leans back on the pillows. Her gauzy white gown blends with the gauzy netting that's draped over the head of the bed. Her hair is a blazing halo around her face. She smiles at me, her eyes a little sleepy, her lips stained purple. Beautiful. "I've never met a girl like you before, H.F. Having you for a friend is like having a best girlfriend and a boyfriend at the same time."

I guzzle the rest of my wine like Kool-Aid on a hot day. I set my glass on the table beside hers, lean forward, and close my eyes. My lips brush hers for a soft, sweet second, and then I pull away, scared that she's mad.

But she's not. She pulls me back toward her, and this time she kisses me. Her mouth mashes mine so our lips lock together. One of her hands snakes up the back of my neck, and every pore in my skin feels shot through with electricity. When her tongue slips between my lips, I yank myself away, breathing like I've just run a mile.

Wendy wrinkles her forehead. "Are you OK?"

"Yeah," I gasp. "I'm better than OK. I'm just kinda new at this."

"At kissing girls?"

"At kissing, period."

"Well," Wendy says, "I'm not new at kissing."

"I can tell." I lean back toward her. This time I don't let her tongue scare me. I touch mine to it, let them slide around each other, all the time feeling like I'm gonna die from pleasure and knowing that if there's a hell to go to for this, it'll still be worth it.

Seven

When I wake up, Wendy's sitting at her desk with her back turned to me. The clock on the nightstand says 6:48. I prop up on one elbow. "Do you always get up this early on Saturday mornin'?"

She jumps a little, like I scared her. "I couldn't sleep."

"Come back to the bed. I'll pet you till you fall asleep."

When Wendy turns around, her face is all blotchy and swollen up. "I can't come back to the bed, H.F. Not while you're still in it."

I sit up like somebody woke me up by pouring a bucket of ice water on me. "Why not?"

Wendy looks at me like I'm the dumbest cow in the pasture. "What do you mean, why not? Do you remember what we did last night, or was that one glass of wine enough to cloud your memory?"

"Of course I remember last night. I'll always remember it."

Tears start spilling out of Wendy's eyes, and she kind of gasps. "Don't."

"Don't what?"

"Don't remember it. Just forget it, OK?"

"Why?" I don't say it, but I'm thinking, *Why should I forget the best thing that's ever happened to me?*

"Because it was a mistake. I mean, my God, I'd never do what we did last night with a boy under my parents' roof. So why did I do it with you? I mean, H.F., if you like girls, there's nothing wrong with that, but you can't expect me to be a...a lesbian just because that's what you are. I don't like girls that way."

"You like me."

"I like you as a friend, H.F., but that's it. What happened last night was...I don't know what it was. I guess I was used to having a boyfriend before I moved here, and I missed kissing and stuff, and well...you were here."

Now I'm crying too, so I know it must be bad, because I don't ever let people see me cry. "So, what...you were pretending I was your boyfriend back home? It wasn't no different than practicin' kissin' on a pillow or somethin'?"

"I didn't say that."

"Well, what did you say then?"

Wendy wipes her nose on the sleeve of her nightgown. "I don't know. I don't know what I'm saying. I'm confused, H.F."

I look at her and know it's me that made her feel this way. I feel horrible and pitiful at the same time, like the monster in the old movie of Frankenstein who just ends up hurting everybody he tries to love. "What can I do to make you feel better?"

Wendy looks right at me for the first time this morning. "Go," she says.

So I go. I pull on my jeans and shoes, grab my bag, and walk out of Wendy's room without saying a word. Thank the Lord, her parents aren't up yet, so I tiptoe through the living room and out the front door, shutting it softly behind me.

Of course, once I'm outside, I realize something that Wendy either didn't think about or didn't care about: I don't have a ride home. Not knowing what to do, I start walking. I walk through Wendy's neighborhood, past all the pretty brick houses with their azalea bushes and flower beds, and shiny new cars in the driveways, and I know in the pit of my belly that I don't belong here. I never belonged in Wendy Cook's neighborhood, I never belonged in her house, and I sure as shooting never belonged in her bed.

Memaw always says there are lines you don't cross. Back

when the miners went on strike when she was living in the coal camp, the worst thing a man could do was cross the picket line. She says you don't cross the line against working people who just want a fair wage.

But the hardest lines to remember not to cross are the lines you can't see. You don't cross the line from remembering where you came from to being something you're not. And that's what I was trying to do at Wendy's—cross the line that separates college-educated people in fine brick homes from people like me. It was just like the yellow tape the police put up on TV shows. It said DO NOT CROSS everywhere I looked, but I crossed it anyway. And now I'm paying for my crime.

Of course, Wendy wanted to cross that line too. I felt it last night when she kissed me, when we were crushed so tight against each other, nothing could separate us. But when she woke up this morning, the line she crossed was glowing like it was made out of neon, and she had to put it between us once again. Because the line Wendy crossed isn't just the line that keeps poor people away from rich people and ignorant people away from smart people. It's also the line that keeps apart girls who like boys and girls like me. Lesbians. Nobody had ever called me a lesbian until Wendy did this morning, and when she said it, I felt how scared she was—scared because I was one and she might be one too.

There's a little grocery store at the foot of the hill, and I think about digging around in my bag for money to call Bo on the pay phone. Still, I don't think I could face him right now. I'd be too ashamed to tell him what happened. Plus, I'm too proud to look him in the face and tell him he was right—that me liking "Pippi Longstocking" was nothing but a useless crush, and nothing's come out of it but pain for us both. I walk past the pay phone.

Downtown Morgan isn't exactly hopping with activity. Since they built the big Wal-Mart out by the interstate, people go there to fill their prescriptions and buy their toothpaste instead of at City Drug like they used to. The Wal-Mart even has a money machine, so you don't have to drive downtown to the bank if you need some cash. Now, on early Saturday morning, downtown Morgan looks so dead you might as well start throwing dirt on it.

There's not a soul out, not even the old men who spend so much time sitting on the benches in front of the courthouse that I've wondered if they get their mail delivered there. The only other person I see is the waitress who's come in to open up the Dixie Diner. Through the window I see her slump over a table, setting out the salt and pepper shakers and the ketchup bottles.

Her name is on the tip of my tongue. I remember when she went to Morgan High. Just like my mom did, she got pregnant and dropped out of school. But instead of running off, she married the baby's daddy and stayed here. Her eyes look like a dead woman's, and even though I wish every day that my momma hadn't left me, I also hope that wherever she is and whatever she's doing, she's having more fun than this poor girl.

I feel as sad thinking about the waitress as I do thinking about me. She probably just wanted to have some fun with her boyfriend one Saturday night. But she didn't know that 15 minutes of fun would make her quit school and end up at the Dixie Diner, going home every night smelling like grease and watching the varicose veins pop out on her legs. And me...all I wanted was to act on my love for Wendy, and here I am, more alone than I ever was—and sadder because I got one delicious taste of something I can never have again.

Memaw says people who choose earthly pleasure have to

pay a price for it, and I reckon I agree with her. Except that Memaw was wrong about *when* you pay the price. Hell don't wait till after you die.

By the time I finally make it home, I'm dripping with sweat, and I've cried till my eyes are so dry I can hear them click when I blink them. If somebody was after me, all they'd have to do is follow the trail of sweat and tears.

Memaw's at the kitchen sink, washing the skillet she fries eggs in. She jumps a little when she sees me, and I don't blame her. I know I must look as bad as a dog's breakfast. "Faith, where in the sam hill did you come from? I didn't see a car pull up."

"I walked."

"You walked? I thought your little friend lived plum on the other side of town."

"She does."

"Well, for land's sake, you could've called your uncle Bobby to come get you."

"I felt like walkin'."

"Felt like walkin' three miles as hot as it is?" Memaw says. "You're the quarest child I ever seen."

Before I even think, I say, "You don't know the half of it." I get the jug of orange juice out of the fridge, pour a glass, and drink it in four gulps.

"You want me to fix you an egg?"

"I ate at Wendy's." When I say her name, the orange juice hisses in my stomach like acid.

"Huh. I never woulda thought them college types would be out of the bed so early on a Saturday mornin'. You'd think they was coal miners."

I can't stand to make small talk with Memaw anymore, so I say, "I stink to high heaven. I'm gonna go take me a bath."

"All right, honey. I'll be readin' my Bible."

I walk toward the bathroom, thinking I've escaped, but then Memaw hollers, "Did you have a good time with your little friend?"

I'm glad my back is turned so she can't see the tears in my eyes. "It was OK."

EIGHT

One time Uncle Bobby tried to talk Memaw into letting him put a shower in the bathroom, but she said she'd never took a shower before, and she didn't see why she should start now. "A bathtub should be good enough for anybody who ain't getting above their raising," she said. After all, she had grown up taking her Saturday night baths in a washtub full of water that her momma had heated up on the coal stove.

In a way, I hate getting into the tub, washing off all the places Wendy touched me. Part of me would like to keep her marks on me, so I could dust myself for fingerprints and find the traces of her touch still on me.

But Wendy wants me to forget, so I sink into the water up to my shoulders, even though I know all the soap and water in the world can't make me forget the feeling of her hands on me. The only way I could forget is to keep sinking under the water until I can't breathe anymore.

But I can't do that. If I killed myself, I'd be killing Memaw too. I look up at the needlepoint sampler of the Ten Commandments hanging on the bathroom wall: THOU SHALT NOT KILL.

There's a Bible verse for every occasion in this damn house.

I grab the soap and washrag and start scrubbing myself off as hard as I can, just like when Memaw used to wash me when I was little, like she was trying to scour off the top layer of my skin.

Big tears roll down my cheeks and plop into the bathwater, and I wish I was a girl who could needlepoint Bible verses and believe them, who thought about things like matching her eye shadow to her sweaters, who wanted a boy to ask her to the junior-senior prom. It must be so easy to be a girl like that— to just naturally be what other people want you to be.

But even if I did like boys, I couldn't be one of them girls— not the way I was raised. Girls like that are raised by two parents who planned on having them and fixed up a nursery while they giggled about the stork getting ready to come.

No stork brought me. I was pushed out between the skinny legs of a frustrated 15-year-old girl who took one look at me and turned tail and ran the first chance she got.

Those stupid, shallow, happy girls never know what it's like to be unwanted. Not like me—unwanted by Wendy, by my own mother. There's only been two people in my life who've wanted me to be a part of theirs: Bo and Memaw. And if Memaw knew all there is to know about me, I'm not sure she'd want me either.

The water is getting cold, so I pull the stopper out of the drain and just lay in the tub, feeling the water get sucked down the drain and wishing I'd get sucked down with it.

Since laying in an empty bathtub all day seems like something a crazy person would do, I finally get out and dry off. When I zip up my jeans, I snag a raggedy fingernail on the zipper and tear it to the quick. "Damn," I say, even though I know if Memaw heard me, she'd preach me a sermon on cussing.

I look in the cabinet for the nail clippers, but they're not there. Figures. Memaw's bad about not putting things back where she found them. The older she gets, the more absent-minded she is. One time she lost her dentures, and we finally found them in the breadbox.

She's still reading her large-print Bible in the living room, tracing her pointer finger under the words and moving her lips just a little. "Hey, Memaw," I holler, "where's the nail clippers at?"

She doesn't even look up from her reading. "I had 'em in my room the other night."

Memaw's dresser has handmade doilies and baby pictures of me, Momma, and both my uncles on it. It has a jar of buttons for when you lose a button off your shirt and a plaque with a poem called "Footprints" on it, but no nail clippers. They're not on top of her nightstand either, so I open the drawer.

I guess everybody has a drawer like the one in Memaw's nightstand—full of loose pennies and nubby pencils and old receipts and recipes. If something small has come up missing, there's a pretty good chance it's in that drawer.

The nail clippers are in there, but they're not what catches my eye.

It's an envelope with a postmark from two weeks ago. The return address reads: Sondra Louise Simms, 520 Palmetto Dr., Tippalula, Fla. My mother.

The envelope is empty, and there's nothing that looks like a letter anywhere in the drawer. I grab a nubby pencil and quickly copy down the address on a scrap of paper and pocket it.

Memaw promised me that if she ever heard from my momma, she'd tell me the very second she did. But whatever was in this envelope came two weeks ago, and she hasn't said one word about it. I think of another one of the needlepointed Commandments on the bathroom wall: THOU SHALT NOT BEAR FALSE WITNESS.

NINE

"Heavenly Faith Simms, you've done gone and lost your mind," Bo says. We're sitting on a rock beside Deer Creek. As soon as I found my mother's address, I called him and told him he had to come get me.

"Well, I've lost everything else. I guess my mind might as well be the next thing to go." I take the address out of my pocket and stare at it for a minute. When I raise my head, I look Bo straight in the eye. "Let me put it to you this way, Bo. Who in this town do you trust?"

"You."

"Me and who else?"

"Just you, but—"

"See," I cut him off, "that's just it. You're the only person in this town that I trust. There for a while I thought I could trust Wendy, but you shoulda seen her this mornin', Bo—she turned on me like a mad dog. All my life I thought I could trust Memaw, but…" I hold up the address. "Just look at this. The one thing I want more than anything else in the world, and she keeps it from me. She can say she loves Jesus till the cows come home, but not tellin' me my momma's been writin' to her—that's as bad as tellin' me a lie right to my face.

"Ever since I wasn't no more than a baby, that old woman's told me it's a sin to bear false witness. 'Faith,' she says to me, 'the truth will set you free.' Well, then, how do you explain this?"

Bo looks at the trees, at the rocks, at anything but me. "I'm sure she's got her reasons."

"Yeah, and I'm sure them football players has got their reasons for poundin' your face into the pavement. Don't you see, Bo? You and me—we're all each other's got in this whole damn town."

Bo squints up his blue eyes. "I don't think I know what you're gettin' at."

I stuff the address back in my pocket for safekeeping. "What I'm gettin' at is...with school out next week, what have we got to keep us here? What's to stop us from just hittin' the road and takin' off—"

"To Tippalula, Florida?" Bo looks at me like he's come to see me during visiting hours at the loony bin. "Lord, H.F., how many hundred miles is that from here?"

"You're always sayin' how you'd like to get out of this town and see the world. Well, here's your chance. I just feel like if I could lay eyes on my momma—if she could just lay eyes on me—things would be OK. I mean, what if she's wanted to see me for years and Memaw's been keepin' us apart?"

"Couldn't you just call her or something?"

"I called information while Memaw was out watering her flowers. Her number's unlisted."

Bo gets up off the rock to pace, then trips over a root and sits back down. "Sugar, I know you're upset, but I can't just take off and drive you all over hell's half acre lookin' for your momma. Daddy would beat the tar out of me."

"He wouldn't if he thought you was goin' off for some legitimate reason."

"And findin' your illegitimate mother is a legitimate reason?"

"No." I wince. I hate that word "illegitimate." I've heard teachers and doctors and nurses use it to describe me all my life—like because I was born out of wedlock means I'm not a real person. "Your daddy don't have to know a thing about me goin' to find my momma. You can tell him..." I try to think of a good lie, but like Memaw says, I've always been an honest soul.

Of course, today I'm starting to learn that when you live in a world full of lies, you've got to turn yourself into a liar just to survive.

"I know!" I say. "You can tell him there's a college down in Florida that's offerin' you a full music scholarship. We can even fake up a letter on one of the computers at school."

"Now, why would a college in Florida want to offer me a full scholarship if they ain't never heard me play so much as a note?"

"Think about it, Bo. We're comin' up with a story to tell your daddy. You really think he'll stop drinkin' beer and watchin' ESPN 2 long enough to think up a question like that?"

Bo shrugs. "Well, Daddy ain't exactly the sharpest crayon in the box, that's for sure."

"Exactly. So the story you tell him don't have to be that good."

Bo runs his hands through his hair, which doesn't mess up even one strand. "OK, H.F. Now, I'm not sayin' I'm gonna do this, because I still think you've lost your damn mind, but just for the sake of talkin' about it, what are you gonna tell your memaw?"

"I'm so mad at that old woman, I don't want to tell her nothin'. I just want to go—run off like my momma done. Because, Bo, today I just about see why she done it."

Bo's face gets all serious and hurt looking. "Now, I want you to know, when you talk that way, what you're talkin' about is killin' an old lady. And I don't care how mad she made you— that don't mean the poor old thing deserves to die."

Bo's right. Memaw may have lied to me, but she's also fed and clothed me for the past 16 years. Even though I'm still mad enough to spit nails, I guess I owe her a lie so she won't worry too much. Besides, she lied to me, and one lie deserves another.

"All right, then," I decide, "I'll tell her I'm goin' with you to look at the college—that you asked me to come along because you're a nervous wreck. Of course, Memaw wouldn't want me going nowhere without adult supervision. So I'll tell her..." I stop to think. "I'll tell her you've got an aunt in Knoxville and that we'll just drive as far as Knoxville by ourselves, and she'll drive us the rest of the way."

"Your Memaw ain't like my daddy. She actually worries about you. What if she was to call my family to check out your story?"

I don't even have to think before I answer. "She wouldn't do that. She...she trusts me to tell the truth." My chest tightens because I'm thinking about the china cat with the broke ear. For a second I feel bad about breaking Memaw's trust, but then I remember how she broke mine.

"All right now—and I'm still not sayin' I'm doin' this," Bo says, throwing a rock in the creek, "but if we did do it, what would we do for money?"

"I've still got my birthday money from Memaw and Uncle Bobby. So that's 50, plus I've got a whole milk jug of change I've been savin'—there's got to be at least 15 or 20 dollars in there. How much you got?"

"I've got about 92 dollars put back, but I've had my eye on this jacket in the Casual Male catalog that I've kinda been savin' up for."

I'm not any good at doing math in my head, but I've still got enough sense to know that between the two of us we've got enough money to make it to Florida as long as fine food and luxurious accommodations aren't part of the travel package. "We can do this, Bo! We've got enough money for gas. We can sleep in the car, and a loaf of bread and a jar of peanut butter will hold us till we get to Florida."

"Where, I guess, you're expectin' a home-cooked meal from

your momma—who don't even know you're comin'."

I close my eyes, and I can see Bo and me driving down miles and miles of open road—not the roads of Morgan that always end up somewhere you've been before, but a road that goes on and on for hundreds of miles until it ends at the door of the woman I've been waiting my whole life to see. And who knows? Maybe she's been waiting to see me too.

"So what do you say, Bo? You're always complainin' about how nothin' ever happens in this town. Are you ready for an adventure?"

Bo looks out at Deer Creek and then down at his hands, which are folded in his lap. His face is as impossible to read as some of those fancy books Wendy likes. Thinking about Wendy makes me flinch.

When Bo looks up, he says, "H.F., do you know that the only time I've been out of the state is when I've gone on a beer run across the state line with Daddy?"

Looking at him, I know I've won. This is the hardest time I've ever had trying to convince Bo to do something. Of course, I've never had the guts to do something this big before. "Are you in?"

"On one condition: I don't want to drive down there and drive straight back. If we're usin' my car, then we have to stop when I want to. I know there's intelligent life out there, H.F., and I want to see it. I'll get you to your mother, but I want to take my own sweet time doin' it. Deal?"

He's the one with the car, so there's no arguing with him. "Deal."

"But just so you know, I still think takin' off to find your momma is a harebrained idea. I'm just bored enough to go along with it."

As we drive back up on Deer Creek Road, I almost want to tell Bo just to hit the interstate and keep on driving. I know better, of course. School's not out till next week, and we can't just disappear. We've got to get our money together and our stories straight. In my mind, though, I'm already on the highway, speeding away from Morgan, away from Wendy's anger and Memaw's lies, and heading toward my momma, toward a place where people tell me the truth and love me just the way I am.

Part Two:

The Journey

Ten

Getting away wasn't easy. Last week, when I told Memaw the story I'd cooked up about Bo wanting me to go with him to look at this college, she pushed her plate away and dabbed at her eyes with a paper napkin. "I swear, Faith, it seems like you're always runnin' off to one place or another…first to stay all night at your little friend's, and now you're wantin' to go all the way down to Florida. But I don't reckon I can do nothin' about it. I just have to get used to the idea that you're a grown girl. Lord, I was married when I wasn't much older'n you. I reckon before long you'll be wantin' to run off and get married too."

I told Memaw that was one thing she'd never have to worry about.

All the time I was getting ready, putting my coins into paper rolls so I could trade them in for paper money and folding up my jeans and T-shirts and sticking them inside an IGA bag, I kept hoping Memaw would say, "You know, your mother lives down in Florida. I've got her address. Maybe you ought to pay her a visit."

But she never did. I guess I could've told Memaw I was going to South Carolina or Alabama or some other state, but I figured that by mentioning Florida to her, I was giving her a chance to tell me the truth. She never said a word, though, and by the time I got up this morning, I already felt a thousand miles away from her.

When Bo came to get me, Memaw followed me out to the car, wadding a piece of Kleenex into a tight little ball in her fist. As I was about to get in the car, she reached down the front of her dress and pulled out three 20-dollar bills and held them out to me. I felt guilty—60 dollars is a big chunk out of Memaw's Social Security check—but I pocketed them anyway. She tapped on her cheek and said, "Give your old memaw some sugar," so I kissed her, feeling for all the world like Judas Iscariot.

"Now, you call me when you get to Knoxville so I'll know you got to Bo's aunt's house all right," she said.

"I'll call you."

"Drive careful," she said to Bo.

"I will, Mrs. Simms. Bye now," Bo called. As we pulled out of the driveway and headed down to the street, Memaw half ran alongside the car, waving and crying.

Only now that we're on the interstate can I look behind me without feeling like she's running along behind me in her house slippers.

"Is she still gainin' on us?" Bo asks.

"I believe we've finally lost her," I laugh. "Good God a-mighty, Bo," I say, looking out at the four lanes of highway stretching out in front of us. "I can't believe we're really doin' this."

"Me neither. Half of me's happier than I've ever been, and the other half's a nervous wreck. I keep feelin' like we've forgot somethin'."

"There ain't much to forget when you're travelin' light." Yesterday evening me and Bo went to the IGA and bought a loaf of light bread and a jar of JFG peanut butter. We both agreed what brand we wanted, but we still had to argue for ten minutes over whether to get creamy or crunchy. Bo's the one with the car, so creamy won. We also bought a gallon jug of water. The label says it came from a mountain stream, but I figure it came straight out of somebody's sink.

After we finished at the store, we drove over to the Pilot,

filled up the car with gas, and bought a road map of the United States. I hope we can read it better than we can fold it.

"Besides," I say, "if we did forget somethin', we've got that 60 dollars from Memaw, so we can buy whatever we need." Except for one thing—I reach inside my pocket to make sure my mom's address is still there. It is.

When we cross the sign that says WELCOME TO TENNESSEE, we let out a "Wahoo!"

"I've always wondered if there was more to Tennessee than the state-line beer stores," Bo says.

"What, do you think that after you pass the beer stores, you just fall off the edge of the world and the monsters eat you?"

"For all I've seen of the world, it could be flat," Bo says. "I bet most people in Morgan don't know no different."

The car starts climbing a big mountain after we pass the beer-store exit. My ears pop as we go higher and higher. The interstate is packed with big semi trucks that look down on Bo's little Escort like an elephant must look at a beetle. They all have the names of places printed on their cabs, like Portland, Oregon, and Kansas City, Missouri. "Bo, just think about how much of the world them truckers has seen. Maybe I'll be a truck driver when I get out of school." Of course, Memaw's too scared to let me get anything more than a learner's permit right now, but once I'm not living under her roof anymore, I can get my license. I look up to see the face of the trucker beside us, but his face is so tired and bored that I figure the whole country is just a blur of gray highway and truck stops to him.

"H.F., if you wanna be a trucker, you're welcome to it. Just don't pull your big semi behind my Escort and proceed to crawl up my ass. Drivin' down Deer Creek Road's no preparation for drivin' in this mess. It's like the difference between ridin' a Big Wheel and a Harley-Davidson."

I laugh when I see an exit sign that reads STINKING CREEK. "Stinkin' Creek," I say, "Well, I guess there's worse places to be from than Morgan."

Bo laughs too. "Can you imagine? You'd spend your whole life makin' up names when people asked you where you was from."

We drive on a ways till there's a sign that says SCENIC OVER-LOOK. Right away, Bo pulls over. "What are you doin'?" I holler. "We ain't even been on the road a full hour, and you're already stoppin'."

Bo puts the car into park. "Look, H.F., when you're a truck driver you can drive straight from one place to another without payin' attention to nothin' but the road signs. But I'm doin' the drivin' now, and I ain't a trucker—I'm a tourist. I'm takin' the first vacation of my life, and I aim to see the sights...at least the ones that don't cost nothin'." He swings his door open. "Now, you can come with me or you can wait in the car."

I'm not used to Bo getting on his high horse like this, so I shrug and get out too.

The overlook is scenic, all right. I lean over the guard rail and look at the mountains swelling up before us, all green with their trees' summer leaves. Way down below is a valley sprinkled with little white houses and barns and churches. It puts me in the mind of the little towns that go with toy train sets. I take it all in, then say, "Yep, it's pretty, all right. Well, I reckon we'd better be gettin' back on the road."

Bo doesn't say anything right then, and when I look at him, he's staring down in the valley like he's hypnotized or something. "Look how tiny all them houses is," he says finally. "Can you imagine how tiny the people down there must look? I bet we couldn't even see 'em from up here. All them little-bitty people livin' little-bitty lives."

"Uh-huh," I say, itching to get back in the car.

Then Bo looks right at me. "I don't want to be like that, H.F....a little-bitty person down there livin' a little-bitty life." His eyes are as blue and lit up as the sky. "I want to live me a great big life, not the kind where you spend most of it just scrapin' to put some baloney and light bread on the table and the rest of it sittin' in front of the TV. I want a life with...with music and friends and, oh, I don't know what all."

Me and Bo bicker like an old married couple sometimes, but moments like this, I remember why he's my best friend. I drape my arm around his shoulders, and we walk back to his car.

✗ ✗ ✗

East Tennessee don't look that different from Southeastern Kentucky. There's the mountains all around us and every once in a while exits for little mountain towns, which I figure are pretty much like Morgan...towns that became towns in the first place because of coal mining and now are just dried-up husks put out of business by the Wal-Marts and McDonald's out by the interstate exit.

We promised Memaw we'd call her when we got to Bo's aunt's in Knoxville. Since Bo's aunt is what you might call a work of fiction, we're not exactly sure where to get off when we get there. I can tell Bo is nervous. He keeps squinting at all the exit signs and tightening his grip on the steering wheel. "I ain't used to this big-city drivin'," he says. "Where do you think we ought to go?"

"I don't reckon it matters much, as long as we find some-place we can make a phone call." I see a sign marked DOWN-TOWN and point to it. "Why don't we go that way?"

When we get downtown we see the most amazing thing.

Rising in the sky is a globe made out of what looks like gold glass. It's cut like a gemstone, and the sunlight sparkles off the facets. "Good God a-mighty," Bo says. "Look at that!"

"It looks like one of them disco balls from *Saturday Night Fever*," I say. "Or like a big, round spaceship that's about to take off."

There's a gas station across the street from the big globe, and Bo pulls into it so we can look at it some more. We get out of the car and stand there, gawking.

"Y'all ain't from around here, is you?" The strange voice makes me jump. When I turn around I see it's just the gas station attendant. He looks to be around Uncle Bobby's age. According to the tag sewn on his shirt, his name is John Ed.

"No, sir," I say. "Kentucky."

Bo nods across the street. "So what is that thing?"

"I look at that dadblamed thing ever day of my life," Jim Ed says. "It's left over from the 1982 World's Fair." He grins. "Shoot, I bet you kids wasn't even born in 1982."

"No, sir," I say.

"Well, you didn't miss much," Jim Ed says. "Nobody much came."

"Is that a fact?" Bo says, still staring at the big globe. "Looks like everybody'd want to see something that looked like that."

"You like it, do you?" Jim Ed shrugs. "I never really think about it one way or another. I guess if you look at the same old thing day after day, it gets so you don't even see it after a while. So, was you kids needin' some gas?"

"No, sir," I say. I look around and notice the pay phone for the first time. "We just wanted to use your phone."

"Help yourself," he says and heads back toward the run-down service station.

The pay phone don't look like something you'd want to put

your mouth against, but I pick it up anyway, push zero, and tell the operator I want to make a collect call.

When the operator connects us, Memaw says, "Faith, I ain't been worth a plugged nickel this mornin'. I couldn't wash the dishes nor nothin' for sittin' here worryin'. I've been in my chair all mornin', prayin' to Jesus that you'd get to Knoxville safe."

"Well, we're here safe."

"You at Bo's aunt's house?"

"Uh...yes, ma'am." Something I've noticed about myself lately is that if I tell a lie, I say "uh" a lot. Even if I was a better liar, I don't know how convincing I'd sound right now. From all the traffic whizzing past the pay phone, Memaw must think Bo's aunt lives in a cardboard box in the middle of a four-lane road.

"Could you put her on for me?"

"Uh...I beg your pardon?"

"Could you let me talk to Bo's aunt for a minute? I just want to make sure she's takin' good care of my girl."

"Uh...just a second." In a panic, I drop the receiver so it swings back and forth all crazy. "Bo," I whisper, but it has to be a loud whisper on account of all the cars zooming by, "Memaw wants to talk to your aunt! What are we gonna do?"

Bo's hands fly up in a panic. "I...I...I..."

"Can you get on and talk like an old lady?"

"I most certainly cannot! Look, just because I ain't the captain of the football team, that don't mean you can make me put on a housedress and a girdle!"

"Not so loud, Bo. Memaw'll hear you." I stare at the phone receiver, which is still dangling.

"Excuse me, boys," a voice says, and I whip my head around to face whatever disaster's about to strike next.

But it's not a disaster. It's a sign. A sign in the form of a real, live old lady standing in front of us.

"I'm sorry to trouble you fellers," she says, and as I focus in on her, I realize she must be one of them bag ladies you see on the news sometimes. Even though it's May and hotter than the hinges of hell, she's got on layer after layer of clothes—probably every scrap of clothing she owns—topped off with a blue winter coat that looks like the big one Memaw bought me when I was little. When she looks at us, her eyes are unfocused, like she might be a few bricks shy of a load. "But I've lost my bus fare and was wonderin' if you could give me 75 cents so I can get home?"

My heart hurts because she's asking for so little and because I'd be willing to bet she don't have a home to get to. I glance over at the phone receiver and decide to take a chance. "Ma'am, how'd you like to make five bucks?"

After I give her a quick rundown of who she's talking to (including clueing her into the fact that, all appearances to the contrary, I'm not a boy), I pick up the receiver, suck in my breath, and say, "Memaw, you still there?"

"I was startin' to wonder if you'uns had done gone to Florida."

"No, ma'am," I say. "Here's Bo's Aunt—" I look at the bag lady and mouth, "What's your name?" She gives me her answer, and I say, "Bo's Aunt Iris."

Against my better judgment, I put the phone in Iris's grimy hand.

Iris cradles the phone on her shoulder real comfortable-like and says, "Hello, Mrs. Simms? I'm sorry I didn't get to the phone faster. It's on accounta my arthur-itis. I don't move as quick as I used to." She laughs a little at whatever Memaw says back and kind of whoops, "Ain't that the truth?"

It's funny. Iris was glassy-eyed and spacey when she was talking to us, but now, on the phone, she's as animated as a preacher's wife at a church social. "The younguns got here just fine," she says. "I was just fixin' them a little somethin' to eat...pork chops and macaroni and cheese, a little kale. Nothin' much, mind you, just plain ol' country food. I may have moved to the city with my husband, God rest his soul, but I'm still just a country girl at heart."

Me and Bo are standing there slack-jawed, listening to her talk. "Oh, you're widowed too?" she says. "It's a lonely life, ain't it? Yessir, the only man I've got in my life now is the Lord Jesus Christ."

Bo catches my eye on that one, and I have to cover up my mouth so Memaw won't hear me laughing. Since Iris managed to work the big J.C. into the conversation, I know Memaw will think we're safe with her.

"I'd love to stop by the next time I'm in Morgan," Iris says. "And we'll be real careful on the way down to Florida. I'll tell your girl to call you to let you know we got there all right. Good talkin' to you, honey. God bless you, now."

As soon as Iris hangs up the phone, her eyes glaze back over. I reach into my jeans pocket and peel a five-dollar bill off my roll of bills, then after I think for a second, I peel off another. She shoves both bills in her coat pocket, says, "Thanks, son," and shuffles down the sidewalk.

I look at Iris walking away and then at the gold globe in the sky and try to decide which one is a bigger wonder.

"H.F.," Bo says, "she did a great job and everything, but I can't believe you give her ten bucks when all she was askin' for was 75 cents."

"Bo, I know we ain't got much money, but that little show she put on was worth ten dollars at least. If I could've pulled an Academy Award outta my pocket, I woulda gave her that too."

Eleven

We stop at a rest area outside Chattanooga and eat peanut butter sandwiches. Squirrels circle our picnic table, hoping for a free lunch. I toss them some crusts.

"Don't you be givin' your food away to them little varmints," Bo says. "Just 'cause they've got some fur on their tails, that don't mean they're no better than a rat."

I laugh as I throw more crusts at the squirrels' little feet. "They might as well have 'em. I don't eat my crusts noway."

Bo nibbles at his sandwich, looking kind of like one of the squirrels himself. "When I was little, my granny always made me eat the crusts on my sandwiches. She said they'd make my hair curly. Now, what I want to know is where them little ol' ladies get all that stuff they tell kids?"

"It's a sight the way adults lie to kids," I say, feeling my momma's address in my pocket. "And the thing is, if you lie to a person for years and years, they're bound to find out about it one day." I can tell by the look on Bo's face that he don't care for the way I took his idle chatter and turned it all serious, so to change the subject, I take out the road map and say, "So, Mr. Chauffeur, how far are you aimin' to drive today?"

Bo studies the map a minute, then grins sheepishly. "I ain't never seen a city as big as Atlanta. Hell, Knoxville looked pretty big to me this mornin'. Why don't we stop in Atlanta for the night? And I was thinkin'...maybe, if we like it, we could stay there a day or two, see what it's like to be in a place where they don't roll the sidewalks up at 4 o'clock in the afternoon."

"Stay there a day or two? Lord, at that rate, I could get to my momma's faster ridin' on a turtle's back. Besides, big cities like Atlanta are dangerous. Memaw talks about that all the time. She says the streets just run red with blood."

Bo raises one eyebrow. "And of course, you believe everything your memaw tells you."

I've got to give Bo a point there. Why should I believe anything Memaw told me about the world? Besides, I've got to watch bein' selfish. Bo's the one wearing out the tires on his car, after all. And we do have a full week for this trip. "OK, OK. Tonight and tomorrow in Atlanta...as long as we're back on the road by tomorrow night."

"Yes!" Bo jumps up and down and squeals, which causes some of the people at the rest stop to stare at us. "Oh, H.F.," he says, "we're gonna have so much fun!"

"Yeah," I say, but I'm not sure what kind of fun we're gonna have in a city where we've got no friends and no money to speak of.

Just the same, when we cross the Georgia line, I let out another "Wahoo!" I love the WELCOME TO GEORGIA sign with the picture of a peach so ripe and juicy looking, you just want to take a bite out of it. After we've stopped for gas in a town that seems like it don't have anything in it but carpet outlets in big aluminum buildings, Bo says, "Let's play a game."

"What kind of a game?"

"Let's take turns singin' every song we can think of that's got Georgia in it."

"You're the musical one, Bo. I couldn't carry a tune in a bucket."

"Good singin' ain't the object of the game. The point is to see how many songs you can think of."

"OK." I think for a second, then launch into a croaky version of "The Night the Lights Went Out in Georgia." I sing all the words I know, then sing "dum-de-dum" for a few seconds, then start laughing. "I told you I sucked."

"Hey, that wasn't so bad. It had a lot of spirit. Not a lot of tune, but a lot of spirit." Then he sings "Midnight Train to Georgia," and it's just beautiful, especially the part where he says he'd rather live in his world than live without him. It gives a whole new meaning to have a boy sing it about another boy, you know?

After Bo's finished, I talk my way through most of "The Devil Went Down to Georgia," except I always forget the part that comes before the devil starts playing the fiddle. Then Bo sings "Georgia on My Mind," which is almost cheating because the name of that song's on the WELCOME TO GEORGIA sign, but Bo sings so good, it's hard to complain. I listen to him and look out the window at the low, rolling hills that are so different from the mountains I'm used to. I like listening to Bo sing, and I like being in Georgia. I like knowing I'm two whole states away from Morgan and Memaw and just one state away from my momma.

After a while, we run out of songs. The car's awful quiet, so I say, "Wanna play truth or dare?"

"I never did like that game much."

"Oh, loosen up, Bo. You made me sing even though I sounded like a donkey in labor. Seems the least you could do is play truth or dare with me."

Bo sighs. "OK, I'll play then."

I can hardly think of what to ask him first. It seems like ever since we was little kids, I've done all the talking and Bo's done all the listening, so my head's so full of questions, it's hard to pick one out. "Truth or dare?" I say.

Bo keeps his eyes on the road. "Dare," he says.

It's hard to do anything too daring while you're driving a Ford Escort, but I hadn't really thought of that when I suggested we play the game. I guess I was just hoping we'd take turns telling each other the truth. "Uh...I dare you to honk your horn three times real loud." It's kind of lame, but it's the best I can do under pressure.

Bo honks his horn, and when we pass the driver who was in front of us, a middle-aged guy in a truck with a Confederate flag bumper sticker, he flips us off. "Well, that was certainly fun, H.F.," Bo says. "Did you see the gun rack in that pickup? It's a wonder he didn't blow us to kingdom come!"

I laugh. "It's your turn to do me."

"You never quit, do you? OK...truth or dare?"

"Truth."

"All right, then. You said you and Wendy kissed and stuff when you stayed all night at her house?"

I swallow hard, afraid I might cry. "Uh-huh."

"Did you do more than just kiss?"

I wanted to play the game to find out more about Bo, not to talk about the things I'd hit the road to run away from in the first place. I decide to joke it off, if I can. "I swear, Beauregard, for somebody who plays the piano in church, you've got the nastiest mind I ever seen."

"Truth or dare, H.F."

"OK, OK, you pervert. We did a little more than kiss. We kinda...messed around."

"Was it...nice?"

I pound my fist on the dashboard. "What does it matter if it was nice or not? No matter how nice it was, it ain't never gonna happen again. OK, my turn's over. Truth or dare?"

"Dare."

I can't think of another dare to save my life. "Now, what fun is it for me if you just take 'dare' all the time, and I don't never get to find out nothin' interestin' about you?"

Bo rolls his eyes. "OK, fine. Truth, then."

"OK. Have you and another boy ever done what me and Wendy done?"

"No." He says it real flat, like it's such a dumb question he can barely get up the energy to answer it.

"Well, that was interestin'," I say, real sarcastic.

"That's the thing about the truth, H.F. Most of the time it ain't nowhere near as interestin' as you'd like it to be."

"Well...have you ever thought about doin' somethin' like that with another boy?"

"I'm only gonna answer one question at a time. That's the way you play the game."

"That ain't fair, Bo. You asked me two questions a minute ago!"

"Yeah, but you only answered one of 'em. Truth or dare?"

I'm tired of throwing Bo big, meaty chunks of information about my life when he won't even toss me a crumb. I fold my arms across my chest. "Dare."

For such a sweet-faced boy, Bo can sure turn on an evil grin. "OK, I dare you to pull up your shirt and flash whatever car pulls up by us next."

"What is this fascination with me takin' my clothes off? What are you—some kind of closet heterosexual?"

"Are you gonna take the dare or are you chicken?"

Bo knows me well. Ever since second grade, all you have to do is call me chicken, and I'll do whatever crazy-ass thing is supposed to prove I'm not one. I stand up on my knees in the car seat, and when a light blue van pulls up beside us, I lift up my T-shirt and display my white cotton bra in all its glory. Like I said a while back, I'm not much in the bosom department. My A-cups are half full or half empty, depending on whether you're an optimist or a pessimist, so I doubt I'm giving much of a thrill to...to...I decide to pull down my shirt and see who I've exposed myself to.

I read the writing on the side of the van: SAINT ANNE CONVENT, COLLIERS, GA. Half a dozen old ladies are looking at me like they're condemning me to drop into hell any second. The nun behind the steering wheel floors it, and the van zips away at what must be at least 90 miles per hour.

My face on fire, I sink into my seat. "Bo, that van was full of nuns."

This ain't news to Bo. He's laughing so hard, he can barely keep the car on the road. "You know," he says between giggles, "I always wondered about the kinda woman that'd be a nun. I bet some of them *liked* you flashin' em." Then he collapses again, and I have to reach over and grab the steering wheel.

"I'm glad you thought it was funny." I take my hand off the wheel and sit and sulk for a few seconds, but then I feel a big gust of laughter moving up my throat. I try to pinch my lips together so it won't get past them, but the force is too strong. I laugh and laugh until my stomach hurts, and I'm afraid I'm gonna have to ask Bo to pull over so I can pee.

Finally, when I can talk again, I say, "I can't believe it, Bo. Except for on TV, I've never even seen a nun before."

"Well, you've seen 'em now," Bo says, "and they've seen you."

"I guess there ain't much point to playing more truth or dare," I say, still laughing. "After you've showed your titties to a vanload of nuns, there ain't much you can do for an encore."

TWELVE

"We must be gettin' close to Atlanta," Bo says, hunched over the steering wheel. "This traffic's about to give me a heart attack."

I look at the cars crammed in close to us, listen to the honking horns. "You can't die on me now, Bo. I ain't got nothin' but a learner's permit. Of course, they do say you can drive with a permit if you've got a licensed driver in the car. I wonder if it matters if the driver is dead or ali—"

What I see makes my mouth drop open. I've always heard about big cities with skylines, but hearing's one thing, seeing's another. The tallest building in Morgan has four stories. The buildings in front of us look too tall to be buildings. They look taller than the mountains back home. "Can you imagine bein' on the top floor of one of them?" I say finally.

"Lord," Bo says, "I'd be scared to death. What if the buildin' caught fire? It'd be like that old movie with O.J. Simpson in it...what was that called? *The Towering Furnace?*"

"Shoot, I'd love to go up in one of them." I point to one building that's got a pointy top to it. "Don't it look like King Kong ought to be up on that one?"

"It's somethin', all right. Hey, you want me to take this exit so we can see the buildin's better?"

"Sure."

We drive between the buildings and just about break our necks looking up at them. I know we look like hicks for gawking, and for a second I think we ought to try to appear more sophisticated, but that's hard when you're riding around in a broke-down Ford Escort with Morgan County, Kentucky, license plates.

Pretty soon I stop looking at the buildings and start looking at the people on the street: men and women in suits half running down the sidewalk like they're in a hurry to get someplace important; skateboarding kids about my age with hair dyed the color of the flowers in Memaw's yard, wearing baggy shorts that hang so low their drawers is showing; a man in a dirty stocking cap pacing back and forth and hollering like he's arguing with himself. White people, black people, Chinese-looking people, tan-colored people who could be Mexicans or Arabs or something.

It's not like Morgan, where all you see is white faces, and not only do you know those faces, but you know their daddy's and granddaddy's faces too.

It's only when I look over at Bo and see how tense his body is that I notice the traffic again. A clock on a bank says 5:15, and I think of a phrase I've only heard on TV: rush hour. "You doin' all right, Bo?" I feel selfish. Here I've been, relaxing and enjoying the sights, just like I was riding in a limousine, never giving a thought to the chauffeur.

"Um...I'd be a whole lot better if I could get out of this traffic for a while. I wonder if there's someplace we could stop."

"I'll look for one." We creep along in the traffic for a while, past a Chinese restaurant and a Church's Fried Chicken. I don't know how I feel about the Chinese food, since I've never ate it before, but my belly growls when I think about that fried chicken, especially since I know it'll be peanut butter and bread and water again tonight. It'll be the same tomorrow and the day after, till we get to my momma's house. I wonder if she's a good hand to fry a chicken.

We keep creeping along in the traffic past a hotel that must have 20 stories. A man in a red-and-gold uniform is standing outside the door, waiting for some rich people to walk up so he can open it for them. I've seen hotels like this in movies, where a boy carries your luggage up to your room and a maid turns down your bed for you and leaves a chocolate on your pillow. Shoot, for the right price, she'd probably read you a bedtime story too or crawl in the bed right beside you. It's something to think about, all right, especially knowing that tonight I'm gonna be sleeping in the same seat I'm sitting in right now.

Bo must be thinking the same thing, because he says, "What do you reckon it'd cost to stay in a hotel like that un?"

"More'n we've got...a hundred dollars probably."

"Well, someday I'm gonna stay in a hotel like that. I'll wake up in the mornin' and order eggs Benedict from room service. I don't know for sure what eggs Benedict is, but I reckon I'll find out."

"They don't build them hotels for people like you and me." I bet there ain't one person staying in that hotel whose permanent address is a trailer on the side of a strip-mine-scarred mountain, like where Bo lives. And I'm sure there's nobody in there whose momma took off and left her to be raised by her memaw neither.

"I swear, H.F., you're the most negative person I ever met in my life. There ain't a thing to stop me from bein' one of them people loungin' around in that there hotel. This is America."

I want to say, *Tell that to the boys on the football team who bust your head every chance they get, not just because you're a faggot but because you're a white-trash faggot.* But instead I say, "Call me when you win the lottery." Bo buys a Kentucky lottery ticket every single week of his life, even though I tell him he might as well flush his five dollars down the toilet.

"Maybe I'll call you...if you start bein' nice to me."

We've moved past the hotel now and past some high-rise apartment buildings. Finally, up ahead I think I see a place where we can pull over.

It's a park, I reckon, but it's much bigger than the Morgan

City Park, which is about the size of Memaw's front yard. This park is acres and acres of grass and trees, and it's just crawling with people—people running, bicycling, playing with their dogs.

It's funny: Back home Bo and me can be out in grass and trees whenever we feel like it, and so we always wonder what it'd be like to live where there's tall buildings and excitement. These city people, though, look like they're glad to be away from all that concrete and walking on some nice, soft grass. I guess it's human nature to want to get away from what you're used to.

"Why don't we pull over here?" I say.

We do, and it feels good to get out and walk around. For my money, this park ain't nothing compared to Deer Creek, if sunshine and green leaves is what you're after, but it is fun to watch the people: the purple-haired kid skateboarding, the redheaded woman pushing a three-seated stroller holding three redheaded triplets. For a second the red hair reminds me of Wendy and my throat aches with the memory, but then my sadness is interrupted by the sight of something I never thought I'd live to see: two guys in their 20s, tan and good looking, both wearing sunglasses and cut-off Levi's, walking through the park *holding hands*.

"Did you see that?" Bo says, and of course, I know right that second what he's talking about.

"I sure did. Do you reckon it's safe for them to be carryin' on thataway?"

"I don't know...it looks like they'd get beat up or arrested or somethin'. That one guy, though...the one with the brown hair?"

Since Bo's trailed off, I prompt him. "Yeah?"

Bo's eyes look all dreamy. "I really liked his...his shoes."

It's the closest I've ever heard Bo come to saying he's attracted to another guy. "You see two guys holding hands in public, and what you notice is what one of 'em has on his *feet*? I bet his shoes wasn't all you liked."

"No, really, H.F.! You can tell a lot about a person by the shoes they wear—"

While Bo's rattling on about footwear, I spot the two guys. They're standing under a big oak tree, still holding hands, talking with their smiling faces real close to each other. "Look, Bo. They're over there."

Me and Bo keep watching them, waiting for somebody to say something or do them a meanness, but nobody ever does. Everybody just keeps right on jogging or skating or throwing Frisbees for their dogs. Nobody seems to notice the two hand-holding boys at all. Of all the things I've seen in one day, this is the most amazing.

When the couple starts to walk again, me and Bo follow them. Neither one of us says, "Let's follow those guys"; we just do it like we've got no choice, like they're the Pied Piper and we're the rats. We stay a ways behind them so they won't notice us, and just watch the easy way they touch and talk. One blond woman who's watching her kids play looks at them a little funny, but her little frown is the closest thing to trouble that they get.

"Lord," Bo says, "no wonder the preachers back home always talk about big cities bein' hotbeds of sin and fornication. I reckon you could do pretty much whatever you wanted in a place like this."

I picture myself skipping through the park holding hands with a girl, but then I remember I don't have a girl to hold hands with. All of a sudden, I don't feel like following the happy couple anymore. "Bo, let's set down a minute. Want to?"

Bo looks longingly at the couple for a second, then says,

"That's probably a good idea. We don't want them to think we're stalkin' them or somethin'."

We sit on the grass and stretch our legs in front of us. "You'll find somebody like that someday," I say. "Y'all can stay at that big hotel and eat them eggs you wanted to try. Then you can walk through the park holdin' hands."

"How do you know that's what I want?" Bo says. "Somebody to priss around and hold hands with?"

"Because it's what everybody wants, whether they admit it or not. And you've got a good chance. I blew mine."

"What are you talkin' about, H.F.? You ain't but 16 year old."

"Memaw was about to get married when she was 16. Bo, Wendy was it. Her and me—we just connected, you know? They'll never be another one like her."

"Hey," a voice deeper than Bo's says.

I look up and see two black girls. One—the one who just said "hey," I reckon—is short and full-figured, but muscular looking. She's got on a red plaid flannel shirt with the sleeves cut off and a pair of blue jeans cut off just above the knee. Heavy black boots are on her feet—the same kind Uncle Bobby wears with his work clothes. She don't have much hair that I can see, but what she does have is hidden under a backwards baseball cap.

The girl beside her is taller and darker and thinner—kind of noble looking, like some African princess. She's got on cut-offs too, but they're much shorter than her friend's. Her T-shirt's short too, showing off her flat, brown belly.

Now, here's the part where you're gonna think I'm a bad person. When I see them, I get nervous. Real nervous. You're not gonna believe this, but I've never met a black person before.

I was telling the truth when I said all the faces in Morgan are white. Not one black person goes to Morgan County High because not one black person lives in Morgan County.

There's a story Memaw tells about something that happened before she was born. A bunch of black men had come to Morgan to work on the railroad, and some of the white men in town got to drinking and got all riled up talking about how black men were taking white men's jobs. The drunker they got, the madder they got, until they finally got their guns, rounded up the black men, and forced them into boxcars and out of town. That was in 1919, and as far as I know, there ain't been a black person living in Morgan since.

Memaw says anybody who'd treat other folks that way, no matter what color their skin is, ought not to be allowed to call himself a Christian. She's right, but I'll go further than that: I don't think a person who'd do another person that way should be allowed to call himself a human being.

So when I look up and see the faces of these girls staring at me, I feel ashamed—ashamed of how the people in my home-town acted back in 1919, ashamed of how they act even today. But behind that shame, there's something else: fear. Not fear that these two girls about my age are some kind of danger, but a fear of saying the wrong thing, the fear that comes from try-ing to figure out a way to talk to somebody who's different than you. Since I don't know what else to say, I finally just repeat what was said to me: "Hey."

"Ain't seen you 'round here before," the girl in the baseball cap says. Her voice is almost as low as a man's. "Name's Denise, but everybody call me Dee." She nods at the tall girl beside her. "This here's Chantal, and—" She whips her head around. "Laney, where you at, girl?"

"Back here." Dee and Chantal move apart, and I see a girl standing a couple of feet behind them. She's a white girl, but she's not like any white girl I've ever seen before. For one thing, she's got an earring stuck through her nose, which I reckon must be downright nasty when her sinuses start to bothering her. Her hair's cut all lopsided and is bleached blond going back to black. Even though it's sticky hot, she's got on a black leather jacket covered in zippers. But underneath it she's got on this skimpy black lace top that looks like underwear. From the waist down, though, she's dressed the same as Dee, in cut-off jeans and black clodhoppers. She nods at us and sucks on her ciga-rette. I can tell she's trying to look tough.

"I'm H.F., and this here's my friend Bo."

"Where y'all from?" Chantal asks. "You talk cute."

"The Bluegrass State," Bo says. " 'Course, the part of the state we're from, most of the grass you see's the green kind you smoke."

Dee and Chantal both crack up at that. Even Laney lets down her guard long enough to smile a little. That's the thing about Bo: When it comes to real personal conversations, he won't tell you a thing about himself. But when it comes to chit-chat, he can't be beat.

"Y'all brother and sister?" Chantal asks.

"Nope, just friends." I don't know why I said it that way— "just friends"—because I've always hated that expression. It makes it sound like friends don't mean nothing compared to family, but I don't think that's true. I mean, I love Bo better than any real-life brother I could've ended up with.

"Kentucky, huh?" Dee says. "Well, you a long way from home. What happened—your folks kick you out?"

I try to imagine Memaw ordering me to get my things and go. "What do you mean?"

"You know," Dee says, like she's explaining something to a dull-witted kindergartner, "because you're queer."

I wonder if we ought to run, if Dee's trying to pick a fight with us. If she is, we'd better run. Even without her friends, I bet she could beat the living daylights out of Bo and me.

When I look over at Bo, he's frozen like a possum waiting to become roadkill.

"Dee didn't mean nothin' bad by that," Chantal says while I'm still trying to figure out what to do. "She just wanted to know if the same thing happened to you that happened to her."

"You got kicked out of your house?" Here I'd been feeling sorry for myself all these years on accounta my momma leaving me, but shoot, at least I've always had a roof over my head.

"Sure did," Dee says. "Of course, I wasn't livin' in no mansion...just a fallin'-down hole in the wall. Shit, you needed a baseball bat to beat the rats off. I never thought my momma give a shit what I done. Most of the time she was out drinkin' anyway. Then one night she come home drunk off her ass, you know, and starts yelling at me how I'd better not get pregnant young like she done. I said, 'Momma, you ain't got to worry about that. I'm a dyke.' And the next thing I knew, she throwed all my clothes out the door with me behind 'em."

"Lord God a-mighty," Bo says. Me, I can't say nothing.

"Even a momma don't love a queer," Dee says. "My brother out on the street sellin' drugs to junior high kids, but Momma don't mind that so much—says at least it bring some money into the house. I figure bein' a dyke ain't like bein' a dealer, 'cause bein' a dyke don't hurt nobody. Momma didn't see it that way, though."

"Same shit happened to me," Chantal says, grabbing hold of Dee's hand.

"Yeah," Dee says, "but you had more to lose than I did—a daddy with a job, a momma that stayed sober, a nice apartment."

Chantal shakes her head. "No point in talkin' about what you lost after you've lost it. Sometimes I wish my little sister hadn't showed Momma and Daddy them poems I wrote, but then I think if I hadn't lost my family, I never would've found Dee."

Dee and Chantal kiss. Seeing them like this out in public makes me shy, and I look down so I won't feel like I'm spying on them. I don't look over at Bo, but I know he's looking down too.

After the kiss is over, Chantal says, "Laney's the one you oughtta talk to, though. She's the rich girl—got kicked out of a mansion in Marietta."

"Which means I'm not a rich girl anymore, no matter how often you homegirls call me one." Laney drops her cigarette and stomps on it with her heavy boot. "But, yeah, I'm from the 'burbs. College-educated parents, big-ass house, full-time housekeeper, the whole shooting match. But then one night my mom didn't knock before she came into my bedroom where I was with my girlfriend, who, incidentally, was tied to my bed." Laney looks right at me and grins. Her lips are painted what Memaw would call "harlot red." "An ostrich feather and a squeeze bottle of honey were involved."

I feel my face burn red because of what Laney's saying, because I realize there's one thing that could've made the situation with Wendy worse: if one of her parents had walked in on us. Of course, I have no idea what Laney's talking about with the ostrich feather and honey. Since I've never done nothing with honey except spread it on a biscuit, I say, "So, did your parents kick you out?"

Laney's forehead wrinkles up. "Yeah and no. They gave me a choice, but it was the same kind of choice as if I held up a sharp stick to your face and said, 'Which eye do you want to keep?' " She looks at her chewed fingernails for a second, then says, "They sent my girlfriend home. Then, after they'd talked to their minister, they called one of those bullshit family conferences that's supposed to make you feel like something you say might matter. They told me I was sick and they wanted to help me...that if I wanted help, there was this place they could send me to—this Christian counseling center in, God, where was it? West Virginia? Someplace fuckin' awful, I know that much. I could go there, and they'd 'rehabilitate' me—naturally, they didn't say 'brainwash,' even though that's what they meant—and after that, I could finish high school at this fundamentalist Christian academy, since public school was obviously a bad influence on me."

"So what did you say?" I ask.

"I said, 'What if I don't want help? What if I think I'm fine, and you're the ones who are sick?' And my dad said, 'Then you're on your own.' I grabbed what I could carry and hitched a ride to the city."

"We do all right," Dee says. "Sleep outside sometimes, sometimes on people's couches."

Chantal grins. "For a few weeks we stayed in this home these Christian ladies run, but then they caught me and Dee sneakin' into bed together, and they busted Laney for smoking."

Laney rolls her eyes, which are lined with black makeup. "It was the same ol' shit, you know? 'If you're gonna live in my house, you're gonna obey my rules.' Well, fuck that! The weather in Atlanta's great about 80% of the time. I don't need a roof over my head that bad!"

"Preach it, sister!" Dee laughs.

"Usually me and Dee don't have much use for rich white girls," Chantal says, "but we like Laney because she's got an attitude problem. At least that's what them Christian ladies told her."

Dee must realize me and Bo have hardly said a word the whole time they've been talking, because she says, "So that's our life story. What you got to say for yourselves?"

I wish I could do something for these girls whose lives are so much harder than mine—wish I could take them with me to Florida and let my momma be their momma too. While I'm standing there wishing I had something to give them, Bo says, "So...do y'all want a peanut butter sandwich?"

Chantal smiles. "Crunchy or creamy?"

Thirteen

It's funny: When I first saw Dee and Chantal, I was scared about what to say to them on accounta them being black, and I didn't know what to think of anybody who'd wear a getup like Laney had on. Then, after they started telling me about getting throwed out of their houses, I started feeling sorry for them—the same way you feel sorry for starving children on TV. I couldn't get over the fact that these girls were homeless.

But now, as we sit on the ground after we've finished our peanut butter picnic, I'm not scared of Dee and Chantal and Laney, and I'm not so quick to feel sorry for them either. While we ate, Dee asked Bo and me to tell them about where we're from.

So we told them about Morgan—about how it's all white people and everybody knows everybody else, how you can't swing a cat without hitting a Baptist church, how there's just one movie theater with only one screen and the movie only changes every two weeks. We talked about how after school we usually just drive around on the back roads, because there's nothing else to do.

And you know what? After we told Dee and Chantal and Laney all that, they felt sorry for *us*. "That's pitiful, having to live in a hellhole like that," Dee said.

Laney just lit a cigarette and said, "I'd slit my fuckin' wrists."

So I guess you ought to be careful who you feel sorry for, because they just might be feeling sorry for you.

I was stupid to be afraid because Dee and Chantal and Laney look different—I might as well have been one of the snooty girls on the Morgan cheerleading squad for thinking that way. Dee and Chantal and Laney are different the way Bo and me have always been different. Different from—what is it Laney says?—"the hets." No matter where we're from or what we look like, we're the same kind of different.

Even though we're sitting under a tree and it's getting dark, you can't hardly hear the regular night sounds like crickets and frogs for all the noise of the city. Laney shucks off her leather jacket, folds it up to make a pillow, and lies back on it, her arms stretched over her head. Her boobies kinda spill out of the black lace top she's wearing, and I notice she's got a little black spider tattooed on her left one. It looks like a black widow.

"Shit," she sighs, "being broke and underage in Atlanta isn't much better than being back in Cripple Creek or Pig Butt Pass or wherever you're from, H.F."

"Morgan," I tell her.

"Whatever," Laney sighs, flipping over to her stomach. "Not a goddamn thing to do."

"Oh, this would be the time of night when Laney starts bitching about not being able to get into the clubs," Chantal says.

"What clubs?" Bo asks, and I wonder if he's picturing those nightclubs they've got in old movies with fancy clothes and little lamps on every table. Knowing Bo, I bet he is.

"You know," Laney says, "clubs with drinks and dancing and women." She looks at Bo. "Or in your case, men."

Even if the half dark, I can see Bo's face turn red.

"Well, I don't drink," Dee says, "and I don't want to pay no ten bucks to dance on a dance floor no bigger than a welcome mat. Plus, I've got all the woman I can handle right here." She gives Chantal a squeeze.

Chantal pecks Dee's cheek, then lifts her arm to look at her wrist. "Damn," she says, "my watch busted a month ago, and I still keep looking at my wrist like it's gonna tell me what time it is."

Bo grins. "H.F., remember when we was kids and if you'd ask me the time when I didn't have a watch on, I'd look at my wrist and say, 'It's a hair past a freckle'?" He rolls his eyes. "In fifth grade, that's some great humor."

Of course, Bo does have a watch on—an expensive sterling silver one he saved up for six months to buy. "I ain't gonna wear no Timex watch just because I live in a Timex town," he said when he showed me the picture of the silver watch in the JCPenney catalog. I glance at the watch on his thin wrist. "It's 10:35," I say.

"We'd better make ourselves scarce soon," Dee says. "The park closes at 11. Of course, we sleep here half the time anyway. We just have to find a place that's kinda outta the way."

"Hey, H.F., you guys got a hotel room or anything?" Laney lights up a cigarette. I wonder how she can live on the street and still afford to smoke.

Chantal puts her hands on her hips. "Girl, you think they'd be hangin' out in the park with us if they had a room over at the Hyatt Regency?"

Laney shrugs. "Never hurts to ask."

"Well," Bo says, "we was plannin' on sleepin' in my car. There ain't much room, but y'all can cram into the backseat if you think you can fit."

X X X

Bo parks the car on a tree-lined street of old houses people have fixed up real nice. Laney and Dee and Chantal are squeezed into the backseat so close together, they look like mixed-race Siamese triplets. Dee and Chantal don't look like they mind the close quarters, but Laney keeps trying to scoot away from Dee, even though there's no place to scoot to. "Damn it, Dee, you've got a big ass," she says.

"Your ass ain't so small for a white girl, Miss Thing," Dee snaps back.

Me and Bo are in the front seat, sitting up straight because we can't lean back without squishing somebody's legs. It's definitely not a room at the High Regency or whatever that hotel was called.

"Going to sleep at 11 o'clock...I might as well be living with my freakin' parents," Laney mutters.

"Well, you'd have a more comfortable place to sleep," Chantal says, "if you'd pretend to like boys and love Jesus."

"I know—it's not worth it," Laney says. "I'd rather be who I am than have the comforts of home. It just sucks that I have to choose."

The same question's been running through my head all night, but I've just now got the nerve to ask it. "So, what are y'all gonna do with yourselves? I mean, you can't live like this forever."

"Me and Chantal read the want ads every day," Dee says. "When we can find jobs that'll pay enough for us to get a place to live, we'll be all right. But it's hard to find a full-time job when you're a teenager, 'cause you're still supposed to be in school."

"I hate bein' a high-school dropout," Chantal says, "but the first thing I'm gonna do after me and Dee get settled down is get my G.E.D. I might even go to college one day so I can get me one of those jobs where you get to sit at a desk all day and tell other people what to do. And Dee—she wants to be a chef. You should see this girl let loose in a kitchen sometime. She can *cook*!"

"Well, you girls have fun working yourselves to death," Laney yawns. "I'm gonna find some rich old dyke to take care of me."

For a long time I don't think I'll be able to sleep. Except for that one night at Wendy's, this is the first night I've slept anywhere but in my own bed in Memaw's sewing room. Plus, sitting straight up with one person beside me and three behind me isn't exactly my idea of comfort. It's been such a long day, though...

✗ ✗ ✗

I wake up to see a man's face staring at me through the car window. His beard is a rat's nest of tangles, and his eyes glow crazily in the moonlight. I must yell, because Bo jerks awake. "What is it?"

"That man...in the window." But when I turn my head he's gone.

"Probably just some old drunk," Dee says from the backseat. "The street's is full of 'em. Go back to sleep."

But it's a long time before I can.

✗ ✗ ✗

When I wake back up, the morning sun is blazing through the windshield, cooking me like a hot dog on a grill. My mouth tastes like dirt, and I can smell the sweat soaking my day-old clothes.

"I know a place where we can get cleaned up and get some breakfast," Chantal says.

Of cleaning up and eating breakfast, I can't decide which sounds better. Me and Bo grab a change of clothes and our toothbrushes out of the trunk and follow our new friends down the tree-lined street. It's hard for me to keep up, though, groggy and dry-mouthed as I am. Plus, it's got to be a good ten degrees hotter in Atlanta than it is in Morgan.

"Lord, girls, how much farther is it?" Bo says, sounding like he did the first time I made him walk to Deer Creek. I'm fixin' to melt into a puddle."

"Not far," Laney says. "Just a couple more blocks."

Bo leans over to me and half-whispers, "What's a block?" The girls all hear him and bust out laughing. I reckon they don't know that when you live in a town that's just got three stoplights, you don't measure distance by blocks. If something's pretty close, you say, "It's about as far as from here to the Baptist church." If something is a long way off, it's "a fur piece."

We follow the girls out of the tree-lined neighborhood past a pizza place and a place advertising sushi, which I remember seeing on TV once is fish that Japanese people eat raw. Now, why would you want to do that when you could fry it up in some cornmeal? I'm glad when we keep walking past the sushi place. No matter how sick I am of bread and peanut butter, I'm not ready for raw fish.

Next we come to this brick building with all these books I've never heard of displayed in the window. The neat white lettering on the window reads, OUT LOUD BOOKSHOP AND CAFE. Hanging over the door is a big rectangle painted with stripes in all the colors of the rainbow. "That's pretty," I say.

"Yeah, that's how you know it's a place for queers," Dee says. "It's got the rainbow sign."

"The rainbow sign," I say after her. The last time I heard the words "the rainbow sign," they were coming out of Memaw's mouth. I haven't thought about it for years, but there was this song Memaw used to sing to me when I was a little girl: "God Gave Noah the Rainbow Sign." It was about the rainbow God sent to tell Noah that He would never destroy the world by flood again. It's funny: I loved that song when I was little, but I had forgot all about it till just now.

"You comin' in, H.F.?" Bo says.

"Oh...yeah."

The store's almost empty. Over at a cluster of tables by the window, an older man is sitting drinking coffee and reading a newspaper. But that's it for customers. The walls are lined with bookshelves, and books are displayed on tables up front. I glance down at one big book that's got a picture of two women, naked and kissing, on it. I jump backwards.

"What's the matter, H.F.? Never seen naked women before?" Laney is laughing.

"Not...not in a book like this."

She grins. "Well, I guess y'all don't have a queer bookstore down in Hooterville, do you?"

"You mean...all these here books are about people..."

"Like us," Laney says. "All kinds of books: fiction, nonfiction, photography, *erotica*." She smiles on that last word, and I look down to keep from making eye contact, but that just makes me have to look at the naked women on the book again.

Instead I look over at Bo, who's spotted some book with a picture of a muscle-bound guy with a policeman's helmet and no shirt on. Poor little Bo's face is so red it's almost purple.

"Come over here, y'all," Chantal says.

We follow her and Dee over to the counter where you can order coffee. A tall, skinny, light-skinned black man is messing around with some kind of fancy coffeemaker. A white girl with the shortest hair I've ever seen on a female is putting bottles of juice and water into a cooler. I wonder what my hair would look like that short.

When the black man looks up, he says, "Why, good morning,

Miss Chantal. You'll be needing the key to the women's room, I presume?"

Chantal looks over at Bo, who's staring at his expensive shoes. "And the men's room key too."

"Oh!" the man behind the counter kinda yelps. "You and your friends have picked up a boy! I didn't know you had it in you." He hands the women's room key to Chantal and holds out the other one to Bo, whose hand shakes as he takes it. "Just look at those hands," the man says. "You're an artist, am I right?"

"A...a...musician," Bo sputters. "I play the flute."

A smile spreads over the counterman's lips. "Ooh, honey, I bet you do!"

Bo runs for the men's room like a scalded dog, with the man behind the counter laughing fit to bust a gut.

The short-haired girl looks up from putting bottles in the cooler. "Levon, you're awful. You scared the hell out of that boy."

"I may have scared him," Levon says, still laughing, "but he liked it, just a little."

With Bo gone and Dee and Chantal locked in the women's room doing heaven knows what, I start walking past rows of bookcases, looking at the names of all these writers I've never read anything by. A couple of them I might have heard about in school...Willa Cather rings a bell, and Oscar Wilde. But mostly as I run my eyes over the names of the writers, I don't recognize them any more than if I was running my eyes over the pages in the Atlanta phone book. When I end up in the same aisle as Laney, I say, "I need to read more. I'm downright ashamed of how ignorant I am. Except for homework, I ain't cracked a book since I read my way through all the Nancy Drew books in the Morgan Elementary School library."

Laney shoves a book at me. "Well, you can start by reading this."

I look down at the page she's opened it to. It's a poem.

"Adrienne Rich," Laney says, like that's supposed to mean something to me.

I start reading the poem, and it's obviously one woman talking to another about how she loves her. And when Miss Rich starts talking about her "cave"...well, I'm no English scholar like Wendy's dad, but I think I've got a pretty good idea what she's talking about. The poem's beautiful, but it makes me feel all hot and flushed and awkward, especially since I can feel Laney's eyes on me. When Chantal and Dee come over to tell me it's my turn to use the bathroom, I'm glad.

As soon as I shut the bathroom's hot-pink door behind me, I strip off my sweaty clothes. After I've taken care of what always needs to be done first thing in the morning, I run the sink full of hot water. Using the store's bottle of liquid soap and a handful of paper towels, I wash off as best I can—hands, face, armpits. After I've let the hot water drain out, I stick my sweaty head under the faucet and rinse it off. I put on a clean T-shirt and panties, brush my teeth, and pull my jeans back on. I'm not clean enough to pass muster with Memaw, but at least I don't smell like a billy goat.

When we turn the bathroom keys back in, Levon says, "And now I suppose you'll be wanting to be fed."

Before anybody can answer, the girl at the cooler starts tossing us these little plastic bottles of orange juice, which somehow we all manage to catch...even Bo, who always ducks when somebody throws a ball to him in P.E.

"Oh, Lordy," Levon says in a loud voice that sounds like Prissy in *Gone With the Wind*. "It's the big boss man. I sho' hopes he don't see me givin' away free food to these po' chillun."

I turn to look at the muscular, bald-headed white man who just walked in through the EMPLOYEES ONLY door. He covers his eyes with his hands like the monkey who sees no evil. "I see nothing. And I certainly don't see any of my employees giving away merchandise."

Levon hands us each a big muffin wrapped in cellophane. "There you go...muffins for the little ragamuffins."

We thank him and take our food outside. Memaw always says she never took a handout in her life, and I probably shouldn't have just now. But I'm hungry, and the muffin is crumbly and moist, with real blueberries. The orange juice flows down my parched throat like liquid sunshine. I close my eyes, drink it down, and think of Florida.

FOURTEEN

We wasted half a tank of gas today driving around Atlanta—
me and Bo and Dee and Chantal and Laney—looking at the
baseball stadium and the skyscrapers and the windows of stores
where we couldn't afford to buy nothing. Seeing the big city is
fun, but it's kind of sad too. It's like being a kid in candy store,
except the man who runs the store says, "Look at all this stuff,
kid. Ain't it great? Well, none of it's for you."

Now we're back in the park because Dee said that it being
a Wednesday, Preacher Dave would probably come by, and if
we play our cards right, we won't have to eat peanut butter for
supper again tonight.

This whole thing is making me nervous, though, standing
around, waiting for some preacher to show up. If I'd wanted to
get my soul saved, I'd have stayed back in Morgan. "So who is
this Preacher Dave guy, anyway?"

Laney lights up a cigarette from the pack I'm pretty sure she
stole from Starvin' Marvin's earlier today. "He's your basic do-
gooder. If we agree to sit through one of his fuckin' church services, he takes us home with him and feeds us. Usually he lets
us shower and sleep there too. His house is *huge*...it's almost
worth going to church just to get to stay there."

All my life Memaw's been trying to drag me to church, and
when I finally get away from her, strangers start trying to do the
same thing. When I think about all the hours I've been forced
to wear a stiff dress and sit in a hard pew and listen to some
man tell me how I'm gonna burn in hell, eating stale bread and
peanut butter and sleeping in the Escort don't sound that bad.

Just as I'm about to say peanut butter sounds fine to me, a car pulls up in front of where we're standing. It's a fancy, shiny black car with lots of silver trim. Bo nudges me. "That's a Mercedes." He breathes the words more than he says them.

Do I really need to say that nobody in Morgan drives a car like that?

The window rolls down—it's the automatic kind, of course—and I see that the driver is a middle-aged guy, balding, with a gray-and-black beard. He's got a gold hoop in his ear, which kind of surprises me, on accounta him being a preacher. "Evening, ladies," he says, then notices Bo and adds, "and gentleman. So, Dee, Chantal, Laney...are you going to introduce me to your friends?"

"This is H.F. and Bo," Chantal says, "from Kentucky."

"Kentucky!" Preacher Dave exclaims. "Where in Kentucky?"

"No place you've ever heard of," I say.

He smiles, and I've got to admit he's got a nicer smile than most preachers I've met. When Memaw's preacher smiles, it's just another way of him saying, *You're going to hell and I'm not.* "Try me," Preacher Dave says.

"Morgan," I say.

"Yes...Morgan." Preacher Dave rubs his beard. "About 30 minutes over the Kentucky state line...there's a little Baptist college there, am I right?"

"Yessir," me and Bo say together, like he just did a great magic trick or something.

Preacher Dave laughs. "I know my Kentucky geography pretty well. You two wouldn't happen to have heard of a little burg called Pine Knob, would you?"

"Where the Pine Knob Coal Company is at?" I say.

Preacher Dave nods. "That's the place. I was born and raised there, God help me. When I was your age, every morning I'd wake up with the same thought: *I've got to get out of here.*"

"Me too," Bo says, and when I look at him, he looks like he's hypnotized.

"Of course you want to get out of there...a young man like yourself. If you don't, you're just going to turn into the town fairy, swishing down Main Street while everybody whispers behind your back."

"Pine Knob had one of them too?" Bo sounds amazed. I'm pretty amazed too.

I look at Bo and say, "Cricket Needham."

"Oh, is he the Good Fairy of Morgan?"

"Yessir," I say, "he's the mortician."

Preacher Dave hoots with laughter. "God bless the poor little sod! In Pine Knob it was Peter Cotton, the florist, surprisingly enough. Peter Cotton...with a name like that, you can imagine what torments he endured." He takes a breath, then says, "So...Bo and H.F., which one of you is which? I had no idea people in rural Kentucky were giving their children such gender-neutral names these days."

"They're not," I say. "H.F. stands for Heavenly Faith, and Bo's short for Beauregard."

Preacher Dave throws his head back and laughs. "Let's hear it for rural Kentucky, with guns for the boys and God for the girls. Still, Heavenly Faith is a beautiful name, even if it is a bit hyperfeminine for a handsome young woman such as yourself."

I look down at the grass. Nobody's ever called me handsome before. To tell the truth, I never thought you could use that word to describe a girl.

"So," Preacher Dave says, "here's the deal. I am in the habit of taking Dee and Chantal and Laney to Wednesday night church services with me. Dee and Chantal are remarkably good sports about it and even sing along with the hymns. Laney rolls her eyes and bites her nails and resents the fact that she can't light up a cigarette right there in her pew." Preacher Dave smiles at Laney, who smiles back like she doesn't really want to but can't help herself. "You two brierhoppers are welcome to join us, but I have no idea how I'm going to squeeze all of you into my car."

Before I can even say thanks but no thanks to his invitation, Bo says, "I've got a car. If you drive real slow, me and H.F.'ll follow you."

I know Bo's trying to concentrate on following Preacher Dave's Mercedes, but I can't help pestering him. "Well, the last dadblamed thing I thought I'd be doin' on this trip was goin' to church."

"Me too, but I like him. Don't you?"

"Yeah, but up till I found my momma's address, I liked Memaw fine too. But I'd rather roll naked in a bed of poison ivy than go to church with her. Besides, what if it's one of them churches that tries to 'cure' people like us?"

"I don't think the girls would agree to go to a church like that."

"They live on the streets, Bo. It's no tellin' what they'd do for a free meal."

"Well, what about you, H.F.? Was you really wantin' another peanut butter sandwich tonight?"

"Not particularly."

"All right. Then hush and let me drive."

Preacher Dave's church is a little yellow brick house. The sign outside says METROPOLITAN COMMUNITY CHURCH, which seems weird to me. All the churches I'm used to seeing are Baptist or Church of God or maybe Catholic. "Community Church" don't seem like it says much about what kind of a church it is.

It's only when I get inside that I start to catch on to what kind of a church it is. On the left, as you come in the door there's a big flag with the rainbow sign I recognize from the bookstore, only this time it's in the shape of a triangle. But here's the peculiar thing: In front of the rainbow-striped triangle is a big gold cross.

It's hard for me to say how I feel seeing these two signs mixed together. All my life I've heard gay people preached against as perverts, and now finding out that there's such a thing as a church for gay people...well, it's awful to say, but it feels like I just found out that the Ku Klux Klan started accepting black members and working for racial equality.

"H.F., you all right?" Bo asks, and I realize I've just been froze right there, staring at that flag.

"Yeah, it's just that...I ain't never been in a church like this before."

Bo does that thing he does where he kind of puckers up his lips and blares his eyes. "Really? Well, me...I go to gay churches all the time. Ain't you heard of that gay church back home, out in Hoot Owl Holler?"

I can tell Bo's in a good mood, because he's teasing me. "Yeah, what's it called—the Fire-Baptized, Foot-Washing, Snake-Handling, Tongue-Speaking First Homosexual Church of Hoot Owl Holler?"

Bo laughs. "You wanna go sit down?"

We scoot into a pew next to Dee and Chantal and Laney. The organist is playing, and Laney already looks bored, gnawing on her nails and scooting around in her seat. She puts me in the mind of a squirmy little kid.

For the first time in my life, I'm sitting in church and I'm not bored. I can't get enough of watching the people. Two rows in front of us, there's this pair of old women sitting together. They've got to be Memaw's age at least. One of them has real short gray hair and is wearing a button-down shirt; the other has her white hair done in soft curls and looks like she could be one of the old ladies in the Morgan Methodist Church, except that a Methodist Church lady would never be cuddled up with another woman like that.

In another pew, there's a pair of guys with matching bald spots, which strikes me as kind of sweet. "His and his" hairlines.

When the preacher gets up to talk, it's not Preacher Dave. Instead it's a woman. Have you ever heard anything to beat that? In Memaw's church, women can't do nothing but teach Sunday school and bring covered dishes for dinner.

The woman preacher's pretty too. She's got short, wavy blond hair and has on one of them shirts with a collar like Catholic priests wear. I can't stop staring at her, and I can't stop thinking, *She's a woman, she's a preacher, and she likes girls just the same as me.*

We sing a hymn, which isn't as peppy as the jumping-Jesus music at Memaw's church, and then the preacher woman starts talking. And do you know what? Nothing she says makes me mad or hurts my feelings. She reads from the Bible about how Jesus helped the woman at the well even though everybody else thought they were too good to have anything to do with her. She talks about how people in the church help people with AIDS and cancer, and teen runaways, which I know is true because I'm sitting next to three of them. She says it's important that we follow Jesus' example and help all the people we can. Now, it seems to me that whether you believe in Jesus or not, there'd have to be something wrong with you if you disagreed with the idea that you ought to help folks.

And do you know how long the sermon takes? I timed it by Bo's watch: 15 minutes. Memaw's preacher couldn't say "kiss my foot" in 15 minutes.

After the service, all these people come up to shake our hands and say they're glad to see us. Dee and Chantal and Bo and me smile right back at them and shake their hands, but Laney stomps off in her big clodhopper boots and says she's going outside to smoke.

When Bo and me are following the Mercedes to Preacher Dave's house, I say, "So, what did you think?"

"I think if they wanted me to sing in a church like that, they wouldn't have to pay me."

"Well, their music sure could use some peppin' up, that's for sure."

Bo shakes his head back and forth. "A church for queers. H.F., I swear to God, at this moment, I really feel like I've seen it all."

But as soon as we hit Preacher Dave's house, I know that me and Bo haven't seen it all, because up until this second we've never seen where a real rich person lives. We're not talking a brick, ranch-style house, which is what passes for a rich person's house in Morgan. This house looks like it came straight out of *Gone With the Wind*—white columns, green shutters, a big yard full of azaleas and magnolias. Dee and Chantal and Laney walk on up to the porch like it's just like the house they grew up in, but me and Bo stand there like we've been pole-axed.

"H.F. and Bo, you are witnessing every little gold digger's dream," Preacher Dave says. "I married an old fag from old money. And would you believe he's a doctor, to boot? That's why I can flutter around all day doing good deeds. Shoot, I'd probably join the Junior League, if they'd let me." He motions us toward the house. "Come on in. Don't be shy. I'm just a good ol' boy from Pine Knob, remember?"

The inside of the house takes my breath away. I've heard of

crystal chandeliers, but this is the first time I've ever seen one in person. "You'll be interested in this, General Beauregard," Preacher Dave says, pointing at the huge painting hanging above stairs that look just like the ones Rhett carried Scarlett up. "That picture of Robert E. Lee was hanging there when we bought the house. It'd been there for generations, so we couldn't bear to take it down. Instead we decided to add some new medals to the good general's jacket." I look at Lee's jacket and see they've painted two buttons onto his lapel: One is a pink triangle, and the other has a raised black fist on it.

"I thought I heard you come in." I look away from the painting and see a tall, silver-haired man who looks like an aging movie star. He leans down to kiss Preacher Dave. "Sorry I was too late for church," he says. "Kidney stones."

"My honey's a urologist, bless his heart," Dave says. "Not everybody knows it, but the foundation of this house is built entirely of kidney stones. So," he says brightly, "Chinese for dinner?"

Bill goes to order the food, and Dee and Chantal and Laney have already taken their shoes off and piled up in what Dave calls the family room, in front of the biggest TV I've ever seen.

"So," Dave says, "would my fellow Kentuckians care to help me in the kitchen?"

Bo gets out silverware for everybody while I take the candy-colored dishes out of the china cabinet. Preacher Dave calls the dishes "Fiesta ware," which strikes me as funny...to call a plain old dish something that fancy. Did I mention that the danged kitchen's about the size of Memaw's whole house?

"What did you think of church?" Preacher Dave says, filling glasses with ice that comes right out of some kind of spout on the refrigerator door.

"You didn't preach," I say.

He laughs. "I'm not really a preacher. The kids just call me that because I drag them to church all the time."

Bo looks up from the silverware drawer. "I never knew there was churches for...for..."

"For us?" Dave says. "Well, think about it. What did Jesus say in the Bible about homosexuality? Not one word. Now, sure, homosexuality is prohibited in the Old Testament, but so is wearing mixed-knit fabric and eating shellfish. And I don't know about you, but I've seen plenty of supposedly devout straight Christians wearing polyester and chowing down at the Red Lobster."

A real Chinese man brings the food right to the door, and after Bill pays him, we sit down to eat. The food is good and real different from anything I've ever ate before. When Memaw cooks vegetables, she cooks them till they're good and done, which means you could practically pour them in a glass and drink them. The vegetables in the Chinese food don't seem like they've been cooked hardly at all. They're still crunchy.

"So, girls..." Dave says. He's sitting at one end of the long dining room table, and Bill's sitting at the other. "What I want to know is why you three aren't living in the place I found for you. I was downright shocked to see your winsome little faces in the park today."

"Got kicked out," Dee says around a mouthful of Chinese food.

"Let me guess," Dave says, "you and Chantal couldn't stay out of each other's beds, and Laney couldn't keep her mouth shut."

The girls laugh.

"Well, I was actually going to call you at the halfway house anyway," Dave says, dipping himself some more of that chicken stuff that's called "moo-something." It seems like if it's called "moo," it ought to be beef. "I was talking to my friend Robin the other day. She and her lover run Myrtle and Hortense's, that trendy restaurant that serves nouvelle '50s food. Meat loaf sandwiches with goat cheese..."

"Tuna noodle casserole, served with a side of irony," Bill says, and Dave laughs.

"Anyway," Dave says, "I was talking to her about y'all...and particularly about Miss Dee's culinary aspirations. And, well, she and her lover have a one-room garage apartment they don't use. She said y'all would be welcome to crash there if you wanted and maybe come help out a few hours a week at the restaurant, washing dishes, bussing tables, that kind of thing. For pay, of course."

Dee and Chantal jump up and hug each other like they've just won the big money on a game show, and then they run over to hug Dave, till he says, "Come on now, girls. I'm a gay man. I can't have women crawling all over me."

"You gonna live with us too, right Laney?" Dee says.

Laney pushes her plate away. "I'll think about it."

I swear, I can't figure that girl out to save my life.

After we eat, Dave and Bill give Bo and me a tour of the house. When we hit the music room, I think Bo's gonna die from happiness right on the spot.

"A grand piano!" He's been trying to act like he sees fancy stuff like Dave and Bill's every day, but when he sees that shiny black piano, I guess he just can't contain himself anymore. "Not a baby grand neither! A full-size one—I swear, it's the prettiest thing I've ever seen."

"Do you play?" Bill asks.

"Yeah, but I couldn't on this one. You should see the old upright I practice on in the school music room."

"Please play something," Dave says.

Of course, Bo can't resist. He plays this classical song the band leader at school gave him the sheet music for, and of course, now he's got it memorized. Bo only has to play a song through twice, then he knows it by heart. The song's beautiful, but it makes me sad too, because I think of Wendy that night at her house, when she played for her parents and me.

"Wow, you're really good," Dave says, and Bo blushes.

Pretty soon Bill and Dave have gotten out this big box of sheet music, and Bo starts playing these songs that sound like they're from old movies or something. Before you know it, they're all three singing, and the sound of it lures Dee and Chantal and Laney away from living room to listen.

"Get a load of us," Dave says. "We're the Three Tenors."

"We look more like the Three Graces," Bill laughs. "Three generations of queens coming together to sing you their favorite show tunes."

Bo doesn't even bat an eye when Bill calls him a queen; he just keeps right on playing. For the first time, he's in good company.

Fifteen

I just had the best bath of my life. The bedroom Dave and Bill put me in has a bathroom right next to it, the prettiest bathroom I've ever seen. The big, claw-footed tub is painted the color of the inside of a cantaloupe, and all the towels and rugs are fluffy and green.

Well, I filled that big old cantaloupe full of hot water and this bubble bath they've got that smells like strawberries. I climbed in with the bubbles up to my neck, closed my eyes, and just lay there, feeling all the dirt and sweat floating right off of me. I washed my hair with this eucalyptus shampoo that made my head all tingly, and by the time I got out of the tub and brushed my teeth and put on a clean nightshirt, I felt like a snake that just crawled out of its dirty, dried-up old skin and found the shiny, fresh skin underneath.

Now I'm laying in a big brass bed with a white fluffy bedspread and a mess of white fluffy pillows. It's like laying on a great big pile of marshmallows. My eyes are closed, and I'm feeling real peaceful when I hear the tapping on the door. "Come in."

At first I don't recognize her. The dark eye makeup and lipstick are gone from her face, which makes her look years younger, like the kid she really is. Her just-washed hair is drying in little curls around her face, and instead of black she's wearing white—a clean, white oversize T-shirt that probably belongs to Dave. "Can I come in?" she says.

"Sure, Laney."

She climbs onto the bed and sits right next to me. "Sometimes at night, when I'm by myself, I get...sad."

"I know what you mean." I say it, but it's just halfway true. I get sad too, and lonely, but even without my momma, I've never been all alone in the world the way Laney is.

"I don't know..." she says, hugging her knees to her chest so I can see she's got boxer shorts on under her T-shirt. "Preacher Dave drives us to that fuckin' church, and I just sit there and think about spending every damn Sunday of my childhood at the Calvary Baptist Church and how all that supposed Christian forgiveness didn't amount to a hill of beans when my parents found out their daughter was a dyke."

"Have you ever talked to Preacher Dave about that?"

"Oh, sure, I've talked to him about it. He said, 'You were raised in hate, Laney, but you can be saved by love.' I told him when he feels the urge to talk like that, he should just needle-point it on a pillow instead."

I think about all the needlepoint sayings at Memaw's and laugh.

"But I don't want to talk about me." Laney stretches out her legs and leans back into the pillows. "I want to talk about you."

"Yeah? What do you want to know?"

Laney smiles, which is something she should do more often. "How many girls have you been with?"

City girls sure don't beat around the bush. I start to say "one," but then decide I don't want to open up the can of worms that was my friendship with Wendy. Plus, I don't know if what me and Wendy did together would fit Laney's city-girl definition of "being with" somebody. "None," I say.

Laney's mouth drops open, then she laughs. "None? You're kidding! But...you do like girls, right?"

"Sure."

Laney flips over on her side so she's laying there like a pinup girl. A pinup girl in boxer shorts. "And...do you like me?"

"Sure, I like you, Laney. You...you..." I don't know what the sam hill I'm trying to say—except maybe "You confuse the living daylights out of me"—but I don't get the chance to say it because Laney starts kissing me. It's not a shy, little getting-to-know-you peck either. Her mouth is open, her lips are wet, and the tip of her tongue touches mine.

"I wanted you the second I saw you," she whispers when we pull apart. "You wiry little butch, you."

I have no idea what a wiry butch is—it sounds like some kind of dog to me—but I've got no time to ask questions because Laney is on me like a duck on a june bug, kissing me and sliding her hands all over me. I keep feeling like I ought to be doing things to her, at least at first, but I figure she knows what she's doing and I don't, so I might as well lay back and enjoy the ride.

The Laney who holds me and kisses me is so different than the chain-smoking, tough-talking street kid I met yesterday. It's crazy to think of, but Laney's like an M&M. She's got a hard shell, but if you can melt it away, what's inside is soft and sweet. As I watch her drift off to sleep, I wish she didn't have to live in a world where gay kids have to grow a hard shell to survive.

✗ ✗ ✗

When I wake, Laney has already gotten up, so I get dressed and go downstairs. Dave and Bill and Dee and Chantal and Bo are in the kitchen, eating coffee cake and fruit. "Pull up a chair, H.F.," Dave says.

"Where's Laney?" I think I already know the answer—or the only part of the answer that matters: She's not here.

"She's taken off somewhere," Dave says. "She wasn't in her room this morning, so heaven knows where she's gotten herself off to."

"Probably down to Little Five to do her special kind of shopping...the kind that don't take any money," Dee laughs.

But I'm not laughing. Tears are burning my eyes. "She...she wasn't in her room last night either."

"Oh, my God!" Dave is up and putting his arm around me. "You adolescents and your raging hormones! If I thought there was any danger of you two getting together, I would've warned you—"

I shrug my shoulders to get loose from his hug. "Danger? Warned me?"

Dave leads me to a chair. "Oh, what I just said sounded too melodramatic. I'm sorry. Laney's a good kid at heart—I'm sure you saw that about her too. It's just that she's been hurt so many times. If she feels herself getting close to somebody, she runs away. I guess she doesn't want to put herself in a position where she can be hurt again. Dee and Chantal can back me up on this."

"Oh, yeah," Chantal says. "How many girls has she hooked up with and dumped just since we've been hanging with her? There was that girl Megan. Then Stephanie..."

"Don't forget Crystal," Dee says.

"Stop." I can't make my voice any louder than a whisper.

"It's OK," Bill says. "She always turns up again sooner or later. Maybe she'll be back in a couple of days and you can talk."

I'm already out of my chair and, in my mind, out the door. "Well, I really don't have time to wait on her. See, I've got somebody waitin' on me right now...my momma, in Florida. Bo, are you about ready?"

"Ready?" I think Bo would just as soon stay with Dave and Bill for the rest of his life.

"To go?" I say, wiping tears on my sleeve.

"Don't you want to wait a while?" Bo tries. "Maybe she just went out for cigarettes or something." I just look at him until he says, "I'll get my things."

In just a few minutes, we're hugging Dee and Chantal and Dave and Bill goodbye. Bo presses a scrap of paper into Dave's hand. "You write me, you hear?"

"I promise," Dave says, and gives Bo a quick kiss on the cheek.

And just like that, we're in the car and on the road again, even though I feel like I left a big, bleeding hunk of my heart in that white, white bed at Dave and Bill's house.

✗ ✗ ✗

Red dirt and kudzu. It's all I've seen since we left Atlanta. Red dirt and kudzu blurred by the tears welling up in my eyes. "You wanna talk about it?" Bo says.

"Not really."

"You didn't fall in love with her, did you?"

"Not exactly. It's just…Bo, my whole life has been nothin' but women leavin' me. First my momma, then Wendy, now Laney…" My throat closes up, and no words will come out for a few minutes. When it opens enough for me to speak again, I say, "I don't want to talk about it."

I close my eyes and hope that when my momma sees me, she'll welcome me like she never was gone. Then maybe I'll be OK.

"So," Bo says, "you wanna talk about me instead?"

I don't even open my eyes. "Huh?"

"You wanna talk about me instead? You know how you're always sayin' I never open up, never talk about myself. Well, I'm doin' it right now, right here—right outside of LaGrange, Georgia, I'm openin' up to you. Ask me anything you want."

But my heart still feels like a boulder in my chest, and I can't think of anything but how sad I am. "I...I can't think of nothin' to ask you."

"Well, I'll tell you what, H.F. I'm gonna do you a favor and talk anyway, because I don't know...I'm in the mood to talk about myself for a change. Now, you can listen to me or you can set there feelin' sorry for yourself—it don't make no difference to me."

I sit up, a little rattled. Bo never talks to me straight like this—well, maybe "straight" isn't the word. "I'm listenin'," I say.

"Good." Bo's real quiet for a minute. He watches the road a while, then he says, "I couldn't get to sleep last night. I was layin' in the softest bed in the prettiest room I've ever been in, wide awake. Maybe the room bein' so pretty was why I couldn't sleep. My eyes just didn't want to stay closed for lookin' at how pretty everything was. Anyway, after a while, I got up and went down to the kitchen. I thought a glass of milk might help put me out, you know.

"So I go downstairs, and Dave's sittin' in the livin' room, readin'. I tell him I got up for a glass of milk, and he says, 'I'll get us both some,' and he leaves and comes back with this black, lacquered Oriental-lookin' tray with milk and oatmeal cookies on it. H.F., we stayed up talkin' till 3 o'clock in the mornin'. He told me about growin' up in Pine Knob and about his first boyfriend in college and about how he met Bill. They've been together 18 years. Can you believe that? Anyway, he just talked and talked, and me, I just sat there and listened, till finally, he says, 'Bo, you haven't told me a thing about yourself.' I say, 'There ain't much to tell,' and he says, 'Well, I do have you figured right, don't I? I mean, you do like boys, don't you?'

"Well, we set there for a long time—for whole minutes, probably—without me sayin' anything, until finally I hear myself sayin', 'Yeah, you're right. I like boys. Not all of 'em, but

130

some of 'em.' He kinda laughs and says he's happy to hear me say that—that he's proud of who I am, and I should be proud too. And after that, H.F., I told him things I've never told another livin' soul."

The question *Like what?* is in my brain, but I can't muster the effort to say it. My head is so heavy, it's all I can do to hold it up.

"And whether you're listenin' or not, I'm fixin' to tell you one of them things right now." Bo sucks in his breath, then lets it out. "You know how when you asked me if I'd ever done the kinda things with a boy that you'd done with Wendy, and I said no?"

I make my heavy head nod up and down.

"I lied to you, H.F. I'm sorry I did, but I lied."

I whip my head around to face him. Suddenly it's not so heavy.

Bo doesn't look away from the road. "One night in the fall, I was settin' at the kitchen table tryin' to figure out my geometry homework while Daddy was throwin' a fit about there not bein' no cigarettes in the house. He was makin' such a racket that after a while I said, 'Fine, I'll go down the hill and get you some.' I didn't want to waste my gas on gettin' Daddy's ciga-rettes, so I thought I'd just walk to Joe's Little Market—it ain't but a mile from the house. So I got to the store and got Daddy a pack of cowboy killers, and as I'm walkin' out in the parkin' lot, this shiny black pickup pulls up and honks its horn. The window rolls down, and I see it's Craig Shepherd."

"The quarterback?"

"None other. He says, 'Hey, Bo, how you doin'?' and I say, 'All right.' I'm not that surprised he's actin' friendly, because Craig's the only member of the football team who'd be worth pissin' on if he was set afire. And besides, I had sung at the church he goes to a couple of weeks before, and he was real

131

nice to me then...told me he'd just about trade in his football talent for a voice like mine, which I thought was sweet. So he's settin' there in his truck outside Joe's market, and he asks me what I'm up to. I say I just run out to get some coffin nails for my daddy, and he says would I like a ride home. I say sure, figurin' he can let me out at the foot of the hill, since I don't much like folks to see where I live.

"But once we're in the car, he asks me if I want to ride around a few minutes, and I say sure. I know Daddy'll be madder than a wet hen at me for stayin' out so long, but Craig's so good lookin', and I'm flattered he wants me to ride around with him. We end up by the lake, with the truck parked all hid by these trees, and I start gettin' scared thinkin' about how alone we are, and what if the other football players put him up to this and he tries to hurt me? When he grabs me I think, *Here it comes: He's gonna kill me.*

"But he kisses me instead. Hard. H.F., the stars are comin' out, and we're underneath them, kissin' and touchin' each other. It was perfect. I couldn't have dreamed it better. I don't know how much time passed before he said, 'We'd better get you home,' but when he said it, I knew he was right. So he let me off at the foot of the hill like I asked him to, and he said, 'You won't tell nobody about this, right?' and I said I wouldn't. Daddy backhanded me as soon as I hit the door for bein' gone so long. But that was nothin'. Daddy backhands me all the time. At least this time it was over somethin' that was worth it."

Craig Shepherd. I can't hardly believe it. "Bo, I never—"

"Hold your horses, H.F. My story's not done yet. The next day, after band practice, about half the football team was waitin' for me. They beat the holy hell out of me, and for the first time, Craig was right there with 'em. He busted the same lip he'd been kissin' the night before."

"Hey," I say, thinking about our stunt last fall, "that was just before we put the pepper juice on their jockstraps, right?"

"Damn straight. I'd made Craig Shepherd burn down there one way, so I was gonna make him burn another. And someday I hope he'll burn in hell too. So when you sit there throwin' a little pity party for yourself over all the girls that dropped you as soon as you touched them, you better save a seat for me. You're not the only one that's been hurt, H.F. And at least your kinda hurt didn't cost you a trip to the emergency room."

I don't know what to say, so I just put my hand over Bo's on the steering wheel and keep it there a few minutes. If Bo and me have to be on such a difficult road—and I'm not talking about the road to Florida, here—at least we get to go down together.

"Seein' Dave and Bill..." Bo says after a while, "I don't know...I guess it gave me hope. Eighteen years they've been together, H.F. They've been together longer than either of us has been alive. Dave looked at me last night, and he said, 'Adolescence sucks, Beauregard. Just wait...life'll get easier.'"

"Do you believe him?"

"I don't reckon I've got a choice but to believe him. 'Cause, sugar, if things get harder, I ain't stickin' around to see the second act!"

After we cross the Alabama state line, we stop for gas and drag out the road map again. To get to Tippalula, you've got to get off the interstate after the Montgomery exit and drive on the state roads through south Alabama all the way to the Florida line. By the time we make it there, it'll be past dark.

Red dirt, kudzu, and pine trees—the pine trees are the only way you can tell you're in Alabama instead of Georgia. For a while we try the song game again. Bo sings that song about going to Alabama with a banjo on his knee, but my head is too full of people—Momma, Wendy, Laney, and even Bo—for me to remember song lyrics, and so I give up after I can't remember what comes after the first chorus of "Sweet Home Alabama."

We drive down the interstate without saying much of anything. One thing I've learned from this trip is that interstate is interstate no matter where you go. The interstate's kinda like Wal-Mart—it may be designed to make your life easier, but it ain't got a lick of personality.

"Bo, I was just thinkin'..." I say. "Most people's lives is like drivin' down the interstate. It's easy, but it's borin'. People like us, though...our lives is like gettin' off the interstate and takin' one of them little windy roads that goes through the country and little towns. Our road may be bumpier, and it may be hard to figure out where you're goin' on it sometimes, but at least it's not boring."

Bo grins. "You think too much." But I can tell he's thinking about it too.

After a while we get off the interstate and start down a narrow road lined with tall pine trees. Bo's little Escort is the only car in sight.

There's a few houses here and there—falling-down wooden shacks held together with tar paper and a prayer. At one, an old black woman sits on the porch breaking up beans while a half dozen shirtless children play in the sandy-looking front yard. At a country store with an antique red gas pump out front, two old black men sit on a bench, drinking orange pops and talking.

"H.F.," Bo whispers like somebody beside me might hear him, "have you noticed that everybody around here is colored?"

"Don't say 'colored,' Bo. If Memaw says 'colored,' she thinks she's callin' black people what they want to be called. But for somebody your age, sayin' 'colored' is backward."

" 'Colored' is a lot better than what my daddy says." Bo shudders. "I hate that word...that and 'faggot.' But you've noticed there ain't no white people here, right?"

"Yeah, it's kinda weird, ain't it? Feelin' like you stand out because of the color of your skin."

"Especially out here in the country like this," Bo says. "I mean...I didn't mean nothin' bad by mentionin' it. I was just...noticin', you know?"

"I know. I don't reckon there's nothin' wrong with noticin' people bein' different than you, as long as you don't think less of 'em for it."

We drive past a sign that's advertising the birthplace of Hank Williams, and Bo says, "That's the first thing we've seen on this trip that my daddy would get excited about." About a mile later, a green sign points out the directions to Barcelona, Alabama, and Destin, Florida. We follow the arrow that points to Florida. From the best I can judge from the road map, Tippalula is about 12 miles north of Destin.

"I can't believe it, Bo. We're almost there. God, what do you think she'll look like? What do you think she'll say when she sees me?"

"Well, there's only one way to find out, ain't there?"

All of a sudden I feel sick, like I used to get in the car when I was a little kid. I take in a big gulp of air, but it's stale car air. "I'm so excited, I'm about to pee my pants."

"Try not to. I don't think it'd make a very good impression on your momma if she thought you was 16 year old and not potty-trained."

✗ ✗ ✗

The sign says, WELCOME TO FLORIDA, THE SUNSHINE STATE, but the sun ain't shining because it's going on 9 o'clock. I expect to see the beach and the ocean and flamingos and seagulls the second we cross the state line, but to tell the truth, it looks just the same as Alabama.

"Can you believe we've been in three states in one day?" Bo says.

I say I can't, but what I don't say is that except for Atlanta, Alabama and Georgia and Florida could all be one state as far as I'm concerned.

Of course, one thing Florida does have on Alabama is billboards. Bright-colored signs are everywhere, advertising casinos and "resort communities" and restaurants. My favorite, though, is a sign for the Sunshine Show Bar. The gold-colored sign shows a woman's legs in fishnet stockings and red high-heeled shoes. In big red letters it says, JUST 8 MORE MILES TO THE SUNSHINE SHOW BAR, THE PANHANDLE'S TOP CHOICE IN EXOTIC AND ADULT ENTERTAINMENT, and then in smaller black letters it says, DOZENS OF BEAUTIFUL WOMEN PERFORMING NITELY—ALL-YOU-CAN EAT PEEL 'N' EAT SHRIMP.

Sure enough, eight miles down the road, we pass the Sunshine Show Bar. It's a plain white concrete-block building with a few pickup trucks parked outside. A tired-looking bleached-blond woman in cut-offs and a Harley-Davidson T-shirt is going into the building. I wonder if she's part of the exotic adult entertainment. The flashing portable sign in the parking lot says, NUDE NUDE NUDE PEEL 'N' EAT SHRIMP.

"Sure you don't wanna stop and eat some nekkid shrimp before we go see your momma?" Bo asks.

It's a little after 10 when we hit Tippalula, and everything downtown is just as closed as it would be in Morgan at this time of night. Come to think of it, the downtown don't look that different from Morgan. There's a dollar store and a drugstore and a video store and a diner. The only thing that makes it different from Morgan is that the diner is advertising shrimp baskets, and there's a shop selling T-shirts and Florida souvenirs. Why would my momma want to take the trouble to run away from Morgan if she was gonna move to a town that looks just like it?

"H.F., I said what do you want to do? You wanna try to find your momma's house or wait till in the mornin'?"

I wonder if this is the second or third time Bo has asked me this question. I see the sense in it, though. You don't just walk into a person's house unannounced at 10:30 at night, even if that person is your momma. I want to, though. I'm so close to her I can feel her—closer than I've been to her in 16 years.

"H.F., I said—"

"I know what you said." I sigh. "Wait till the mornin', I guess."

"Well, I reckon we'll have to find a place to park for the night, then."

Just outside of town we find a little park. It hardly has any lights, so we sit in the dark and spread some peanut butter onto two heels of bread, which is all we have left of the bread we bought in Morgan. We drink a little bit of our bottled water, which has gotten so warm you could take a bath in it. But there won't be any baths tonight. Not even a bathroom to pee in, since the public restrooms have been locked up for the night. I squat behind a pine tree before I come back to the car, lean back in the passenger seat, and try to sleep.

Sixteen

When you sleep in a car, you don't need an alarm clock. As soon as the sun rises, it blasts through the windows, making my eyes snap open, then close back up in a squint. "We gotta get out of here before we roast alive," I say, swinging open the door.

The park is empty, and now that it's daylight, I can see that it's also pretty ugly. There's just a few scraggly pine trees, and the ground is too sandy to grow much grass.

"Look," Bo says, pointing at a white bird that just swooped down and landed on a picnic table, "a seagull."

I look at the seagull, and he looks at me. He's pretty—pure white with gray-tipped wings. Even though I'm still mad at Memaw, I think of her for a second. She keeps a bird feeder in the backyard and is always staring out the kitchen window at the cardinals and blue jays. I bet she's never even seen a seagull. "Well," I say, "it ain't a flamingo, but I reckon it's still a sign that we ain't in Kentucky anymore."

"That's for sure. It even smells different down here. Have you noticed?"

I hadn't, but I take a good, long sniff. For a second I don't know what I'm smelling, but then I remember it's a smell that Uncle Bobby described to me from his days in the Navy: the sharp smell of saltwater. I start walking toward the smell. "Come on, Bo."

"Come on where? Can't we see if they've unlocked the park bathroom so we can clean up a little first?"

I look and Bo and can't help laughing. He's a mess. His wavy hair is smooshed down on one side where he's slept on it, and his white shirt and tan pants are all wrinkled. As bad as he looks, I know I look worse. "You look great," I lie. "Come on." Without even knowing I'm going to do it, I break into a run.

Bo trots along behind me, panting, "H.F., unless there's a man with an ax gainin' on us, I don't see why we have to be goin' so dadblamed fast."

I run through the patch of pine trees, then I stop. I don't look over to see Bo. I'm too busy staring at what's in front of me. But I hear him beside me, breathing.

The beach is long and white, not tan like the sand in little kids' sandboxes. It curves and dips like a woman's body and stretches to the left and the right as far as I can see. In front of me is the ocean. I say the word again in my head: *ocean*. It's a beautiful word for a beautiful thing, but *thing* seems like such a small word for something that's bigger than I can even imagine. I think about the globe in our history classroom—how all the continents look like tiny islands compared to the hugeness of the ocean. And it's so blue.

"You know," Bo says, "when I was a little kid and I'd draw pictures of water, I'd always make it blue. But I'd never seen blue water before...just clear water in a blue swimming pool. But this...this is blue."

"Like a blue glass marble."

"Like Cal Ripken's eyes."

I take off my shoes and let the sand sift between my toes. And then I'm running again, barefoot, toward the water. I pull my T-shirt over my head, then step out of my jeans. I unhook my bra and shuck off my panties and run into the ocean. My toes squish into the wet sand, and the waves pour over me. When I'm up to my waist, I look around toward Bo, who I keep expecting to holler at me for being crazy enough to take my clothes off. But when I look around at him, he's already got his shoes, shirt, and pants off, and seems to be debating what to do about his underwear. He finally shucks that off too, and runs into the water to meet me.

We swim and splash and play like a pair of toddlers in the world's biggest wading pool. Even if somebody walking along the beach was to see us, I don't think we'd be embarrassed. You don't expect dolphins playing in the water to be wearing clothes, so why should we?

"H.F.," Bo hollers over the sound of the waves, "you know how I said I wanted to live a big life? I think I started livin' it today!"

I wrap my arms around Bo and hug him. All his boy parts are touching my girl parts, but there's none of the spark that I'd feel pressed up against Wendy or Laney. You know how the hateful preachers are always saying that God made Adam and Eve, not Adam and Steve? Well, hugging Bo naked in the ocean, I feel like we're a new kind of Adam and Eve. We already ate the fruit from the Tree of Knowledge, and instead of being punished for it, we learned that the world is big and full of opportunities, and that love is always good: Girls can love girls if they want to, boys can love boys if they want to, and a girl and a boy can love each other as dear friends and nothing more or less. We are naked, and we are not ashamed.

On the beach I put on all my clothes, and Bo puts on his underwear and pants and turns his shirt into a bag for collecting shells. We walk along the shore, picking up nature's free souvenirs. I look up in the sky at a seagull, and suddenly Bo picks me up under my arms and sets me down a few inches away from where I was. "Hey, what was that for?"

"Look where you was about to step."

I look down and see what looks like a clear plastic bag with strings dragging behind it.

"A jellyfish," Bo says. "I ain't never seen one before, but I know about 'em because my cousin got stung by one down in Myrtle Beach. They're poison."

I step back from the little bag; it don't look like something dangerous. "Your cousin...did he die?"

"No. Their sting won't kill you. It'll just make you hurt real bad."

"Well, thanks for savin' me." We walk farther down the beach, picking up more shells, but this time I watch where I'm going.

People are starting to come to the beach. Families with picnic baskets are spreading out blankets. I watch a little girl in a Mickey Mouse hat and sunglasses stand still while her mother rubs suntan lotion on her back, arms, and legs. "Bo," I say, "I think I'm ready to meet my momma now."

In the park restroom, I change into a yellow polo shirt and a clean pair of jeans. The ocean has already washed me clean, so all I have to do is brush my hair and teeth. When I look at myself in the mirror, I look pretty OK. I look like I could be somebody's daughter.

Since Tippalula is about the size of Morgan, Palmetto Drive isn't hard to find. Like you'd think from the name, there are palm trees growing right by the sidewalk, but the houses aren't that fancy. Mostly they're just little white frame houses that put me in the mind of Memaw's. When we get to the house with Momma's address, it's also a little white frame house not much different than Memaw's, except not in as good a shape. The yard needs cutting, and the white paint is chipping off the wood. Memaw's house has aluminum siding. But I don't care what Momma's house looks like. I've had a million different fantasies about her, but not one of them was about her being rich.

Bo parks in front of the house. "You want me to wait here or come with you?"

"Come with me. I'm as nervous as a cat."

I knock on the screen door several times. I'm about to give up and come back later when the door opens. A good-looking shirtless man stands in front of us. He's young, with shoulder-length brown hair and blue eyes, and for a second, in my nervousness, I wonder if he could be my brother. This is stupid, of course; even though he's young, he's still older than me. He stares, waiting for me to say something, till I finally manage to get out, "Does Sondra Simms live here?"

"She might. Depends on what you're after."

He seems like he's as nervous as I am, so I say, "I'm not after nothin'. I'm a friend of hers from Kentucky. I was just passin' through town and thought I'd stop by to say hello."

He looks me and Bo up and down, like he's deciding we're not too dangerous. "Well, she's workin' over at the City Cafe if you want to go see her." As soon as he says it, he closes the door.

"You reckon he's her husband?" Bo says when we're in the car.

"Nah, he's too young. Probably just her roommate. Maybe they're real good friends like you and me."

"Well, he ain't too much like me," Bo says. "If I was about to answer the *phone*, I'd put a shirt on."

The City Cafe is the same place we drove by last night. It's a little nicer than the Dixie Diner on the inside, cleaner and maybe remodeled. A waitress in a powder-blue uniform walks up to us. She's got blond hair, but I still check her name tag on the chance she could be my mother. Her name is Donna.

"Two?" she asks, looking at Bo and me.

"Uh, actually, we're just lookin' for somebody that works here...Sondra Simms."

Donna turns away from us and yells so that everybody in the

Florida panhandle can hear her: "Sondra! A coupla kids up here wanna talk to you!"

When she comes out from the back of the restaurant and walks toward me, it's like a scene in a movie where everything's in slow motion. Customers are looking up from their shrimp baskets and bowls of chili to see what she does, to hear what we say.

She's still pretty. The dark brown hair I remember from her picture is shoulder length now, and permed. Except for a few tiny lines at the corners, her eyes are just like in the picture, coal black and determined underneath their fringe of dark lashes. She's put on maybe 20 pounds over the past 16 years, but the extra padding just makes her look like a woman instead of a girl.

She looks at Bo and me like she's trying to figure out if she knows us from somewhere. Finally, she says, "Can I help you?"

I want to say, "Momma," but Donna is still standing there, and the lunch customers are still staring at us like we're the free entertainment. "Uh," I stammer, "could I talk to you outside for a second?"

She shrugs. "Yeah, but just for a second. I've got customers to check back on. Donna, tell Lenny I'm out smoking a cigarette and I'll be right back, OK?"

We stand on the sidewalk while my mother takes a pack of cigarettes and a lighter out of the pocket of her uniform. She lights one and squints at me through a veil of smoke. "OK, so what do you want? You're too old to be selling Girl Scout cookies."

I had hoped she could tell who I was just by looking at me, but of course she can't. "Sondra," I say, even though it sounds weird to call her by her name, "I'm your daughter, Heavenly Faith."

She laughs a low, throaty laugh. "No shit? Well, your granny saddled you with a hell of a name, didn't she?"

I grin. "Everybody but her calls me H.F."

She looks me up and down. "Well, H.F., you need a makeover about as bad as any girl I ever seen. Of course, you wouldn't know how to fix yourself up being raised by that old woman. Does she still wear that same blue flowered dress to church every Sunday?"

I know the dress she means. "She did till a couple of years ago. It finally got so faded that she give up and bought her another 'un. It's blue with flowers too."

My mother laughs, which makes me feel good. We have things in common, I think. She likes me.

"Well, I guess bein' raised by her, you're lucky you're not walkin' around in a polyester dress too." She looks at me harder, then frowns. "There's not a thing of me in you. I guess you look like your daddy."

"My daddy?" I've never wanted a daddy like I've wanted a momma, but I've always been curious who my father might be. Memaw never will say a thing about who Momma was dating when she got pregnant.

My mother laughs. "Don't look at me, kid. Livin' with that Jesus-crazy old woman in that Jesus-crazy little town made me wild as a buck. I don't remember half of what I did back then. Hell, you'd probably have more luck pickin' out all the men under the age of 40 in Morgan and linin' them up to see who looks most like you than you would askin' me who your daddy is." She takes one last pull off her cigarette, then stubs it out on the City Cafe's windowsill. "Speakin' of men, who's your boyfriend there?"

Bo's been standing there the whole time, and I had plum forgot about him. "This is Bo, but he ain't my boyfriend."

"No," she says, "he don't look like boyfriend material. Well, my five minutes is up. I've gotta get back to my customers."

I don't mean to be rude, but I still hear myself saying, "Look, since we're in town, I was wonderin'...could we maybe stop by your house a few minutes this evenin'?"

She's already opened the door of the restaurant. "Sure, whatever. I get off at 6."

I watch the door close behind her.

Seventeen

We stop at a little grocery store and splurge on Red Delicious apples and cold bottled Cokes and little packs of salted peanuts. We take our snacks down to the beach and stare at the ocean while we eat and drink. Bo and me both empty our packs of peanuts into our Cokes, so that when you turn up your bottle to get a drink, you also get a mouthful of peanuts. The last few swallows of Coke are salty like the ocean. I feel happy.

I keep wanting to ask Bo what he thinks of my momma, but part of me is scared to ask him—scared he might say he don't like her, and then I'd have to be mad at him.

So I don't ask him. Neither of us says much of anything that afternoon. We just listen to the ocean, let it do all the talking.

At 6:30 we head back over to Palmetto Drive. This time my mother opens the door. She's fresh out of the bath, wearing jeans and a T-shirt from some place called Margarita Pete's that says, ONE TEQUILA, TWO TEQUILA, THREE TEQUILA, FLOOR. With her clean face and regular clothes, she looks more like the girl in the picture I've looked at so many times. She holds the door open. "I brought home some shrimp boxes from work. Come on in and eat."

Momma must not love pictures and knickknacks and what-nots like Memaw does. There's nothing hanging on the living room walls but the drab brown paneling. There's not much in the way of furniture either—a secondhand tan couch and chair and a beat-up coffee table with an overflowing ashtray and rings left from glasses sitting on it. Across from the couch, though, is a TV almost as big as the one at Dave and

Bill's, with a VCR sitting underneath it. I know Memaw would throw a fit if she seen this place, but I don't mind it so much. I always figured the kind of mother who cleaned house all the time would also be the kind of mother who'd want me to put on a dress.

We follow Momma into the kitchen, where the guy who answered the door is sitting at a folding card table, drinking a can of Milwaukee's Best. He still don't have a shirt on. "This is Travis," Momma says.

Bo and me say, "Nice to meet you."

Travis mumbles, "Hey."

"The shrimp's on the table," Momma says. "You can just grab a box. We've got beer and water. What do you want?"

"Water," I say.

"Water," Bo says.

"Pussies," Travis says, grinning.

Momma gives Travis a playful slap on the arm. "Now, I told you to behave yourself. Of course H.F. ain't gonna drink a beer. I'm sure her memaw told her that so much as one sip would send her straight to hell. Am I right, H.F.?"

"That's about the size of it. I don't believe it, though." I don't want her to think I'm some kind of religious fanatic just because Memaw is. "I've just never liked the way beer tastes."

"Me neither," Bo says.

Travis looks at Bo suspiciously, like the fact that he don't like beer automatically makes him a fag.

I've never ate shrimp before, and it's real good, except it seems weird to be eating a whole animal in one bite. Momma don't eat much. She just nibbles a couple of french fries, then pushes the box away and lights up a cigarette. She seems nervous, and I think I know why. It's Travis. If he wasn't here, her and me could have a real mother-daughter talk.

"So," I say, "you wanna know anything about anybody back in Morgan?"

She blows out a cloud of smoke. "No."

I want to say, *You want to know anything about me?* but I'm scared of what she'll say.

"H.F. is real smart in school, Mrs. Simms," Bo says. "She don't hardly study at all, but she still keeps a B average."

"So what are you tryin' to say?" my mother says, her voice on edge. "She keeps a B average, but I dropped out, right?"

"No, ma'am," Bo says, backpedaling as fast as he can. "I didn't mean nothin' like that. I just...I just thought you might like to know."

"Huh," she says, getting up and taking two beers from the fridge, one for her and one for Travis. "Why don't we go watch some TV?"

My mother lays on the couch with her legs stretched across Travis's lap. I let Bo have the chair. I sit on the carpet, which feels gummy. We watch two shows, one about paramedics rescuing people that have got beat up or burned. The camera stays right on the accident victims while they jabber away about how much they hurt. The other show is about pets that go crazy and attack people. Nobody in the room talks except during commercials.

During a commercial for some medicine that's supposed to cure baldness, my mother says to Bo, "So who are you anyhow? You're not family too, are you?"

"No, ma'am. I'm just H.F.'s friend. My daddy's Johnny Martin."

My mother's eyes light up. "No shit? Johnny Martin that used to hang out over at the Hilltop Tavern?"

"Yes, ma'am. He still does."

"Oh, yeah," my mother smiles. "I remember Johnny. I had

me a fake ID, used to sneak out of the house and go to the Hilltop all the time. Johnny'd buy me beer—he used to buy all the girls beer, you know. He was a good-lookin' fella. I never could figure out what he wanted with that hangdog wife of his."

Then the show comes back on, and she stops talking so we can all see the toy poodle that caused a door-to-door salesman to have his big toe amputated. Bo sits in the chair, his lips a straight line of rage because that "hangdog wife" of Johnny Martin's is his mother.

By the time the pet show is over, my mother and Travis have drunk two more beers. I told myself I wasn't going to keep track of how much my mother was drinking, but I can't stop myself from counting the cans. Suddenly she picks up the remote, puts the TV on mute, and turns to me. "OK, H.F.," she says, "I give up. I wasn't gonna say nothing, but I give up. Why did you come all the way down here? Because if you want money, we ain't got none."

I feel like she hit me. I almost wish she had. "I don't want money. I just wanted to see you."

She sits up straight. "See, that's what I'm asking. Why? Why did you want to see me?"

Because you're my mother, I want to say, but all I can get out is, "I thought we could talk."

My mother laughs. "About what? About the ass-end of nowhere, Kentucky? About my crazy mother? Look, H.F., I wanted to get out of Morgan the second I was old enough to walk. When I finally did leave, I was gonna do it free, with no baggage. And no baggage means no boyfriends and no babies. You ain't gonna make me feel guilty for leaving, so don't try. You should be grateful I had you at all. The only reason I did was because I was broke and ignorant."

This isn't the way it's supposed to be. When I do talk, I

sound like a whiny four-year-old. "But didn't you ever think about me?"

"Sure. Your granny sends me letters, so I knew you were all right. It wasn't like I dumped you in a garbage can, for God's sake."

I'm trying not to cry. I feel Bo's hands on my shoulders. My mother lights another cigarette. "I mean, I'd understand it if you was some kind of famous teenage model or if you'd won the lottery and you came to find me to say, 'Look how rich I am, look at how great I turned out.' But coming down here the way you are, with your friend the way he is? Are you trying to embarrass me? You and your little faggoty friend want to make me ashamed, to make me feel like it's my fault you turned out to be—"

"You *should* be embarrassed. You *should* be ashamed." I look up and see that Bo has got up out of his chair. "You should be embarrassed and ashamed, because havin' H.F. is probably the best thing you ever done in your sorry excuse for a life, and you don't have the good sense to appreciate her."

I can't believe Bo's stood up for me like that. I'm crying for real now, and when I look up, I'm surprised to see my mother is crying too. "I'm sorry," she sobs. "I didn't mean to say that. It's not my fault I can't be a mother to you...not my fault I have to live in this shithole. You feel so goddamn sorry for yourself because your mommy took off and left you, but what about me? Do you think this is what I wanted? I wanted to be an actress. I was supposed to be wearing evening gowns in Hollywood, not wearing a polyester waitress uniform in the friggin' Florida panhandle!" She looks at us with wet, red eyes. "Say, kids, why don't you stay the night? Me and Travis got an extra room."

"OK," I say, hoping things will get better and hating myself for hoping.

Fishing the last cigarette out of a pack, she doesn't even look up at us. She just says, "It's the first door on the right. Why don't you kids go on to bed?"

I stand up to leave the room because it's what my mother wants me to do. The whole time we've been screaming and yelling and crying, Travis hasn't looked away from the TV once.

I guess it was stupid, but I thought that because my mother was telling us to go to bed, that meant she was going to bed too. Me and Bo are sitting on a mattress on the floor in the tiny spare bedroom, listening to my mother and Travis fight:

"I told you to pick up a carton of cigarettes on your way home from work."

"And what are you doin' all day that you can't haul your ass down to the corner store and buy the damn cigarettes yourself?"

"Oh, ain't this somethin' new and different? You ridin' my ass 'cause I can't find a job."

"You can't find somethin' if you don't look for it!"

"Oh, and you'd know all about lookin', wouldn't you? All that lookin' you do at every man that gives you the time of day...and you can't tell me you don't do more than look. That's how you ended up with that dyke bastard you've got for a daughter."

I put my hands over my ears and rock back and forth. "I can't take this, Bo."

Bo gently pulls my hands down and holds them in his. "Well, that's because it's new to you. I'm used to it. This feels just like home to me."

"She said she was sorry she said them things to me. Do you think she meant it?"

"Oh, sure. They treat you like shit, then they feel bad about it and say they're sorry, and then they forget they was sorry and start treatin' you like shit again."

I'm a damn fool. I had every reason to believe that Sondra would be a lousy mother, but I chose to believe different—like a dog that makes a long, hard journey to find his way back to the master who abandoned him on the side of the road. "Bo, let's go home."

"We will, in the mornin'. But I can't drive them dark country roads at night. It ain't safe."

I don't feel safe here either, but I say, "OK." In the living room, I hear something hit the wall with a thud. I jump.

"I'm gonna go out to the car and get our bags," Bo says. "I'll be right back."

"You can't go out there with them fightin' like that."

"They won't even notice me. They're like a pair of dogs layin' into each other. They won't notice you unless you turn a hose on 'em."

Bo sleeps on the mattress, not stirring no matter how loud the yelling gets. After a while things settle down a little, and I curl up beside him. Then I hear my mother and Travis in their room, my mother crying out and the mattress squeaking. I feel like I know what every night with my mother and Travis is like, beer and TV till they get all riled up, and then two loud activities that start with the letter f. I know that when my mother wakes up in the morning, she'll be glad I'm gone.

I cry quietly to myself, then doze off for a little while. My eyes open as soon as the sky starts to get light. "Bo," I shake his shoulder gently, "let's go." We take turns cleaning ourselves up in the mildewed bathroom, then check the kitchen to see if there's anything we can grab for breakfast. But there's only a case of beer in the fridge and a carton of cigarettes on the counter. Figures. There's nothing in this house that's good for you.

Once we get to the end of Palmetto Drive, Bo starts heading toward town instead of away from it. "Where are we goin'?" I ask. Between my sorrow and lack of sleep, I sound like I'm on drugs.

"Home," Bo says. "But first we're gonna say goodbye to the ocean."

We stand on the white beach, watching the big red ball of sun rise over the blue water. The sky is splashed with soft colors—rose, orange, and yellow—like a watercolor painting. "It's hard to believe anything can be so beautiful," I say, "especially in a world where mommas leave and girlfriends leave—"

"Now, wait just a minute," Bo says. "The way I see it, you should be pretty happy. You've met your momma, and you know you wasn't missin' a thing. Your life's been a damn sight happier without her than it would've been with her. People like your momma and that Laney girl, they're leavers...always movin' on to the next person or the next place, and they'll leave that too. I bet your momma will leave Travis before the year's out, and I bet they's at least a dozen boyfriends that came before him. Leavers leave, H.F. That's just the way they are."

"What about Wendy?" When I was awake crying last night, I was surprised to discover I was thinking about Wendy almost as much as my mother.

"Wendy's different. She's just scared of her feelings. I know what that's like. I lived most of my life that way. But not anymore." Bo looks at the sun for a second, then says, "H.F., someday you'll find a girlfriend who'll stay. And you've always got a friend who will."

I squeeze Bo's hand, and suddenly I get a jolt like I just stuck a hairpin in a light socket. It's a thought and a feeling all at once, and it zips from my toes, up my spine, and finally to my mouth. "Omigod, Bo, I just thought of something. You remember my mother talkin' about your daddy last night?"

"Yeah, everybody from Morgan knows my daddy. Why?"

"Did you see how her eyes got all soft and glittery?"

"Yeah, so?"

"I was just thinkin'... She was hangin' out at the Hilltop when she was 15, lettin' your daddy buy her drinks. What if she did somethin', you know, to pay for them drinks? I mean, what if they went for a ride in his car one night, and—"

Bo's eyes get wide. "Well, Mommy is always accusin' Daddy of runnin' around with loose women—"

"And my mother is definitely a loose woman."

"So, what you're sayin' is it's possible we could be..." He stops talking and looks at me.

I look back at him. We're both tall and wiry like his daddy is, and we've both got blue eyes. His hair's ash blond, but that comes from his momma. We both have the same kind of ear-lobes. Bo and me was born a month and a half apart, so his mother and my mother was both carrying us at the same time, two babies made with the eggs of two different women, but with Johnny Martin as the father.

This is just an idea—there ain't no proof for it—but I know that when Bo looks at me and smiles, he's thinking the same thing I am: It's possible.

EIGHTEEN

"You do look like him," Bo says as we're driving through the sticks of south Alabama. "I'd never thought of it before because I like you and I can't stand my daddy, but y'all do kinda look alike."

I laugh. "Who'da thought that ol' macho, Civil War-lovin' Johnny Martin would end up makin' two queers in one year?"

Bo grins. "We ought to get him a belt with that stamped on it: TWO QUEERS IN ONE YEAR."

I feel nervous all of a sudden. "We're not gonna tell him, are we? I mean, we don't have one iota of proof—"

"Of course we're not gonna tell him. He's the worst father that ever was. But at least you're gettin' a helluva brother out of the deal." Bo looks down at the gas gauge. "God a-mighty, we've been drivin' along talkin' while we're sittin' on empty."

We pull into the old-fashioned gas station we passed on the way to Tippalula. A sign says PAY BEFORE YOU PUMP, so I get my bag out of the backseat and reach for the plastic change purse where I'd stuffed all the money for our trip.

It's empty.

No, I say to myself. *Don't panic.* The money probably just fell out into the bag. I turn the paper bag of clothes upside down on the passenger seat and start digging through it.

"What's the matter?" Bo says, sounding like he's afraid I've finally stopped messing around and have lost it altogether.

"The money. There was $32.14 in here yesterday, and now I can't find it."

"Shit," Bo says. "Shit, shit, shit."

"No, no, it's OK," I tell him and myself at the same time. "It's got to be here somewhere."

"It ain't here, H.F. It ain't here because somebody took it."

As soon as he says it, a picture flashes in my mind: the carton of cigarettes on the kitchen counter in my mother's house. Wasn't that what Travis was yelling about last night? That he didn't have any cigarettes? The case of beer in the fridge was new, unopened. While we slept the pitiful amount we slept last night, somebody took our money and went on a shopping trip. I'd like to believe they just borrowed the money—that they would've paid us back this morning if we'd stuck around, but I don't think that Jesus Christ himself would be charitable and forgiving enough to believe that. "Good God a-mighty, Bo, what in the sam hill are we gonna do now?"

Bo sighs and looks over at the two men sitting on the bench in front of the station. "I guess we can start by talkin' to them men that's been starin' a hole at us the past five minutes."

I look over at the two old black men sitting on folding chairs outside the building. They've stopped their game of checkers to watch us. I suck in my breath and walk over to them. Both of them have soft gray hair and look like they could be somebody's papaw. I pray that they are.

"Hello," I say. "Me and my friend was down here visitin' colleges." I can't bring myself to say "visiting family." "And I was just lookin' in my bag, and I think we've been robbed. I was gonna buy some gas, you see, but now I can't..." My voice is getting higher and out-of-control sounding, "And I don't know what we're—"

"Hold on, missy," the heavier of the two men says. "You got somebody back home to wah you some money?"

"I beg your pardon?" A south Alabama accent is a lot harder to understand than a southeastern Kentucky one.

"To wah you some money? By Westun Union?"

"Oh." *Wire* me some money. "Yeah, I guess so."

The old man takes three one-dollar bills out of the pocket of his coveralls. "Heah. You give this money to Ed to buy you some gas, then you head back thataway about 12 mile to Barcelona. Westun Union's on Main Street."

"Thank you, sir." I'm crying again. "Thank you for bein' so nice. Give me your name and address, and I'll pay you back."

"Don't you worry about it, missy. I ain't so bad off I can't afford to give a little girl three dollars."

Barcelona, Alabama, looks about like Morgan, only a little worse. Maybe the thing that makes it worse is the way people are looking at us. Back in Morgan everybody knows who I am, even if they hate me. Here, everybody's looking at Bo and me with skinny eyes that say, *Who in the name of God are you, and what are you doing here?*

Of course, what I'm doing here is standing at the pay phone outside the Western Union, trying to decide who I can call to wire us money. Memaw would do it, but then I'd have to explain to her that we lied to her, why we lied to her, and why we're in Barcelona, Alabama (and I'm not even clear on that last one myself).

Bo's daddy might send money, but he'd only do it so he could kill Bo the second he got home. Then I have an idea. It's a risk, but it's easy to take risks when you've got nothing to lose.

"Who ya callin'?" Bo says.

"Shh." I know the number by heart. I say my name at the beep and pray that whoever's on the receiving end will accept the charges.

Wendy answers, and I'm prepared to go into a speech about how sorry I am to be bothering her and how I'll never pester her again but that I really need her help. But I don't get a chance to say any of this because she says, "H.F., where in the hell are you?"

"Uh...Barcelona."

"You're in *Spain*?"

"No, Alabama."

"Well, everybody here's worried to death about you...your grandmother especially. She called here last night nearly hysterical. She said you were supposed to call two nights ago and didn't. She called the college that was supposed to have offered Bo a scholarship, and they said they'd never heard of him. She said if you hadn't shown up by this morning, she was calling the highway patrol, so I guess she did."

"Well, tell her to call off the highway patrol. Tell her I'm all right, and I'm sorry." I hate to think how much pain I've caused Memaw. After all, the only reason she kept me away from my mother was to protect me from the same pain Momma had caused her.

"H.F.," Wendy says, so soft I can barely hear her, "I'm sorry too. As soon as I found out you were gone, I knew it was because you were running away from something...from me and how ugly I was to you, most likely. I was scared, H.F. Scared of the way I felt about you and about what that might mean about me. But I've thought about it a lot. I still don't have many answers. I don't know if I really like girls...or if I just like you."

All of a sudden, I don't even care that I'm broke and stranded in Barcelona, Alabama. "You like me?"

"I feel like everything happens for a reason, H.F. And the only possible reason I can think of for moving to a god-awful town like Morgan is so I could meet you. Call me when you get home, OK?"

"Uh...about getting home—"

"Yes?"

"Me and Bo...well, it's a long story, but we're out of money. We're standin' outside the Western Union, flat broke."

"You want me to wire you some money?"

It's hard to say yes because of all Memaw's speeches about a Simms never taking a handout from nobody. "I'll pay you back, Wendy. I swear to God, I will. We just need enough for gas back to Kentucky—"

"Don't get all poor and proud on me, H.F. It's no problem. I've got to get downtown to the bank, then over to the Western Union at the City Drug, so it'll probably take me about an hour. Barcelona, Alabama, you say?"

"Thank you, Wendy. Thank you so much."

"Like I said, not a problem. I'm glad I can do something to halfway make up for how mean I was that morning. Say, my parents are going out of town for a conference next weekend. You want to sleep over?"

I know from how hot my face is that it's turned red. I'm grinning all over myself. "You bet."

I hang up the phone and throw my arms around Bo's neck. "She likes me!" I yell. "She likes me and she's sorry she was mean to me and she wants me to stay all night with her and—"

"Keep it down, H.F.," Bo says, removing my arms from around him. "You can't be yellin' stuff like that in south Alabama. They'll find us danglin' from a tree somewhere!"

I shut up. I can't stop grinning, though.

"Is she sendin' the money?" Bo asks.

"It's true what they say about little gay boys: gold diggers, every one of you." Bo don't laugh, so I say, "She's sendin' it. It should be here in about an hour."

✗ ✗ ✗

Wendy has sent 150 dollars, which makes me wonder if she was going down to the bank to rob it. The first thing we do is go to the Dairy Queen across the street and buy hamburgers and Cokes and ice cream cones. It's the first food we've had all day, and it's so good that I close my eyes when I take my first bite of burger so I can taste it better. When we're done, I look at Bo and say, "Let's go home."

Epilogue

Me and Bo made that trip to Florida 18 months ago, but I still remember coming home like it was last night. Memaw came running out on the porch in her housecoat and slippers, and let me tell you, for an old lady, she can flat *run*. I thought she was going to say, "Why did you lie to me?" or "I ought to tan your hide," but instead she took both my hands in hers and said, "Did you see her?"

My eyes filled up. "Yes, ma'am."

"Well," she said, "I reckon you're satisfied now."

"Yes, ma'am." As awful as meeting my mother had been, I was satisfied. My questions about her had been answered.

"All right, then. Let's not say another word about her. I'll send her a little money from time to time on accounta her bein' my daughter, but I don't want to know what kind of sin that girl's livin' in."

"Yes, ma'am," I said.

I know Memaw and me have different ideas of sin. Memaw would think it's a sin that my mother is shacked up with a man ten years younger than her and that they've got a refrigerator full of beer. I don't care about either of them things, though.

The way I see it, my mother's personal life is her business. The thing that bothers me about my mother is that she's spent every day of her dadblamed life thinking about nobody but herself. To me, that's a sin.

It's hard to understand how a person like my mother could come from somebody like Memaw, who's spent her whole life thinking about what she can do for other people. When her and me went in the house that night, she went right into the kitchen and started heating up the pan of macaroni and cheese she'd made for me as soon as she heard I was coming home.

The next Friday, I stayed all night with Wendy. We had the whole house to ourselves, and for the longest time, we just talked. Wendy said how sorry she was for pushing me away, but she was scared of her feelings, scared of what it might mean to be something other than a straight girl. "I mean," she said, "it's not like I'm not a big enough freak in this town already."

I told her I had something to apologize for too. I had loved her so worshipfully that I had turned her into a perfect goddess instead of a regular person, with doubts and fears. I told her that I promised to love her as a person—a wonderful, beautiful person, but a person just the same.

We're still together, Wendy and me, but we save all our touching and kissing for private. Memaw don't suspect a thing, and right now I want to protect her from what she can't under-stand—maybe because that's the best way to protect Wendy and me too. I like to think that someday, when I'm grown and out of her house, I can make her understand about the way I am, but I don't know if I can. The only person Memaw loves more than me is God, and since she don't go to the Metropolitan Community Church, the God she worships says all gay people are going to hell.

Wendy's parents have been around the block a few more times than Memaw, and I think that Wendy's mom might have at least a clue. She left this book called *Patience and Sarah* out where Wendy could read it. She lent it to me, and I read it too. It was good—kind of like *Little Dykes on the Prairie*.

Wendy says her mom and dad keep mentioning friends of theirs from back in Pennsylvania who are gay. After school's out, Wendy's going to write a coming-out speech and practice it so she can say it to her parents. It's funny she's so nervous, since they've already showed her that things are going to be the same between them. Besides, she's not gonna be telling them anything they don't already know. I figure if it ain't against your religion, it ain't so bad to have a dyke for a daughter. At least you don't have to worry about her turning up pregnant.

At school, it's always Wendy and Bo and me, just like it used to be—eating lunch together, taking all the classes we can together, going to Deer Creek after school when it's pretty. For a while me and Bo talked about going to the doctor and getting blood tests run to see if we're brother and sister. But finally we decided it wouldn't be worth the trouble—we're brother and sister no matter what some test might say. There's more to family than just blood.

Bo and Preacher Dave write each other every week. Dave told Bo that Dee and Chantal are doing real good. Dee's working full-time at that restaurant now, making salads and desserts and pretty good money. Chantal just got her G.E.D. She's got a job at a store that sells hip-hop clothes, and she's applying for night classes at community college. The last time anybody saw Laney was four months ago. Wherever she is, I hope she's OK. And if she's not, it's her parents' fault as sure as if they'd picked up a gun and shot her.

I guess Preacher Dave decided to make Bo one of his little do-gooder projects, because two months ago Bo got a letter from Atlanta State University telling him he'd just won the Desmond Reed Memorial Scholarship, which is given every year to a student with exceptional abilities and who is also openly gay. All Preacher Dave would say about the scholarship was that Bo got a little help from a good fairy.

Bo has begged Wendy and me to come with him to Atlanta after we graduate. It's tempting, but Memaw's not getting any younger, and I don't want to be too far away in case she needs me. She's always done right by me, so I ought to do right by her.

Besides, Wendy got a full scholarship to the University of Kentucky and is gonna be in this honors program they've got for extra-smart people. She told me I ought to apply to UK too, so I filled out an application in study hall one day, halfway as a joke.

I thought I was going to die when I got the letter saying I got in, and Memaw broke down and cried because a member of the Simms family was going to college. Of course, I didn't get put in with the real smarties like Wendy did, and I didn't get a scholarship, but I did get enough financial aid that, with a little help from Uncle Bobby, I can afford to go.

Me and Wendy have asked to share a dorm room. Ain't that a kick in the pants? Straight college boys and girls are always trying to sneak into each other's dorms, but if you're gay, you can live with your lover in your own private bedroom.

This year Bo and Wendy and me have learned the meaning of the word *senioritis*. We've always hated Morgan High any-how, and now when we're in school, we don't hardly pay any attention to where we are because we're too busy thinking about where we're going.

We've just about got all our required classes out of the way, so we're taking the easiest classes we can. I'm taking art, and we're working on these projects that Wendy's mom is going to put on display in the Randall College Art Gallery. The idea is that young people in the community collaborate with old people to make art, so one day a week a bunch of old people—some from town and some from the nursing home—come in and work with us.

I'm collaborating with Memaw. For my part, I'm making a big batik wall hanging with rainbow stripes on it just like the rainbow sign at Out Loud Bookshop in Atlanta. For Memaw's part, she's making a quilted Noah's Ark and all these little quilted animals that are just perfect—you ought to see them. We're going to stitch the ark and the animals onto the big batik rainbow.

I know Memaw takes the story of Noah's Ark and the sign of the rainbow at face value—that it was God's way of saying he wouldn't flood the world again. But I think of it another way. It makes me think of the trip me and Bo made together.

See, the way I think of it, for me and Bo, the world was getting mean, just like it was for Noah, so we climbed into Bo's Ford Escort just like Noah did in his ark, and we took a little trip. Of course, Noah packed his ark full of good people and animals so they'd stay safe from the flood and the mean people. Here's where we're different: me and Bo gathered up our good people along the way. Preacher Dave and Bill, Dee and Chantal, and Wendy, who helped us when we really needed it. We learned that the world isn't just flooded with meanness—that there are people like us loving each other, living happy lives out in the open. Their lives together may be harder because there's plenty of meanness in the world, no doubt about it, but their happiness is probably greater because they can never take their love for granted.

Memaw would say I was blaspheming if she knew I was comparing something in the Bible with my own experience of being queer. But I think the way I do because of who I am: a teenage dyke from small-town Kentucky, raised by my memaw on Bible stories and old-timey hymns. And to me, the rainbow sign God put up in the sky for Noah said pretty much the same thing as the sign I saw at the gay bookstore, at the church, and in the faces and hearts of the rainbow of people who are my gay family: "Here you were, thinking it was the end of the world, when it turns out it was only the beginning."